PUFFIN BOOKS

The
Great
Escape

Megan Rix lives with her husband by a river in
England. When she's not writing she can be found
walking her two golden retrievers, Traffy and Bella,
who are often in the river.

Books by Megan Rix

The Great Escape

megan rix

PUFFIN

PUFFIN BOOKS

Published by the Penguin Group
Penguin Books Ltd, 80 Strand, London WC2R ORL, England
Penguin Group (USA) Inc., 375 Hudson Street, New York, New York 10014, USA
Penguin Group (Canada), 90 Eglinton Avenue East, Suite 700, Toronto, Ontario, Canada M4P 2Y3
(a division of Pearson Penguin Canada Inc.)
Penguin Ireland, 25 St Stephen's Green, Dublin 2, Ireland (a division of Penguin Books Ltd)
Penguin Group (Australia), 707 Collins Street, Melbourne, Victoria 3008, Australia
(a division of Pearson Australia Group Pty Ltd)
Penguin Books India Pvt Ltd, 11 Community Centre, Panchsheel Park, New Delhi – 110 017, India
Penguin Group (NZ), 67 Apollo Drive, Rosedale, Auckland 0632, New Zealand
(a division of Pearson New Zealand Ltd)
Penguin Books (South Africa) (Pty) Ltd, Block D, Rosebank Office Park, 181 Jan Smuts Avenue,
Parktown North, Gauteng 2193, South Africa

Penguin Books Ltd, Registered Offices: 80 Strand, London WC2R ORL, England

puffinbooks.com

First published 2012

010

Text copyright © Megan Rix, 2012
Map and illustrations copyright © David Atkinson, 2012

All rights reserved

The moral right of the author and illustrator has been asserted

Set in 13/16 pt Baskerville. Typeset by Palimpsest Book Production Ltd, Falkirk, Stirlingshire
Printed in Great Britain by Clays Ltd, St Ives plc

British Library Cataloguing in Publication Data
A CIP catalogue record for this book is available from the British Library

ISBN: 978-0-141-34271-9

www.greenpenguin.co.uk

*In memory of all the pets that lost their lives in the
Second World War*

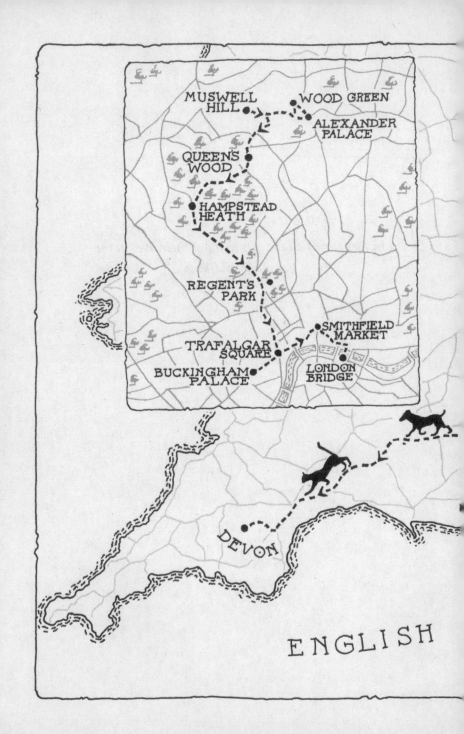

MUSWELL
HILL

WOOD GREEN

ALEXANDER
PALACE

QUEEN'S
WOOD

HAMPSTEAD
HEATH

REGENT'S
PARK

SMITHFIELD
MARKET

TRAFALGAR
SQUARE

BUCKINGHAM
PALACE

LONDON
BRIDGE

DEVON

ENGLISH

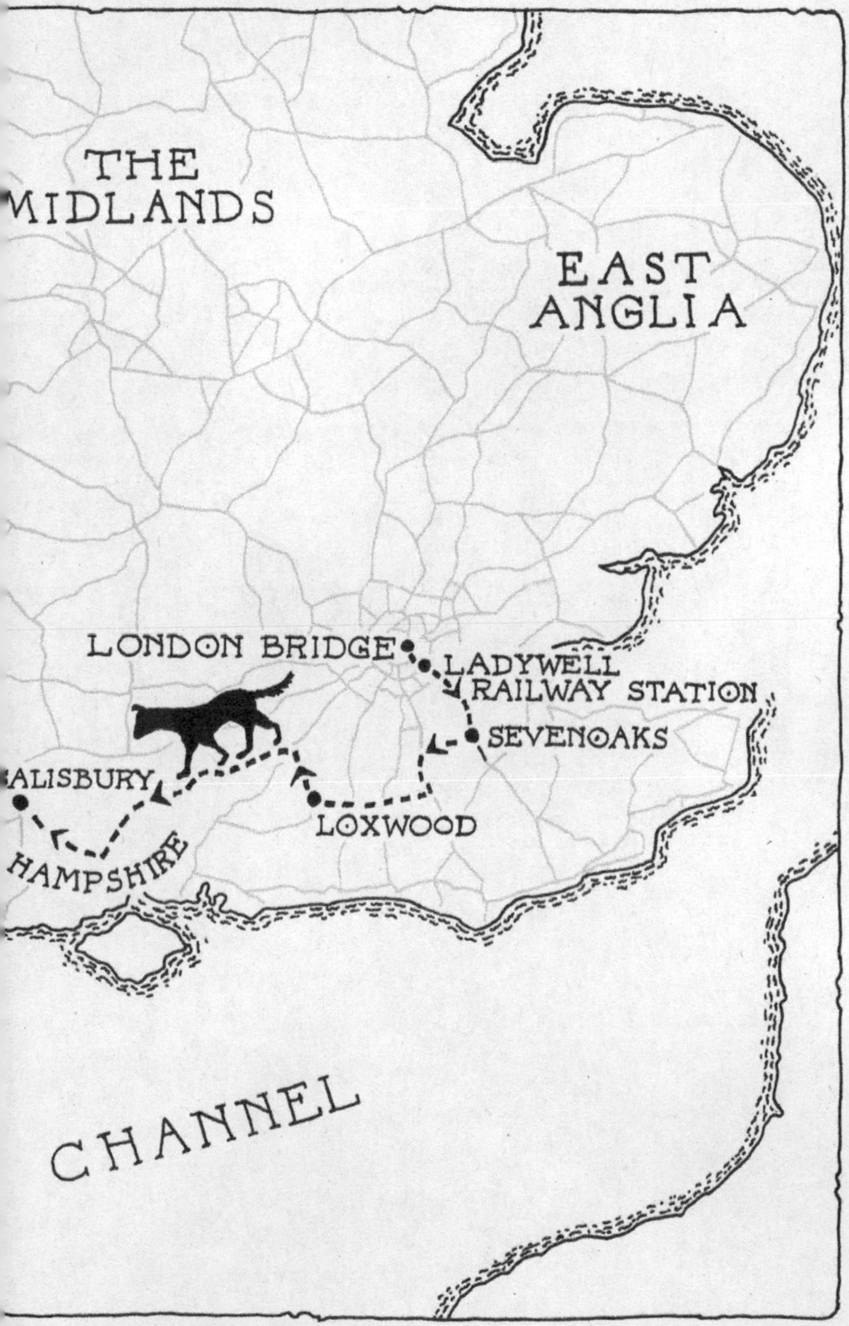

THE
MIDLANDS

EAST
ANGLIA

LONDON BRIDGE
LADYWELL
RAILWAY STATION
SEVENOAKS

ALISBURY
LOXWOOD
HAMPSHIRE

CHANNEL

Chapter 1

On a steamy hot Saturday morning in the summer of 1939, a Jack Russell with a patch of tan fur over his left eye and a black spot over his right was digging as though his life depended upon it.

His little white forepaws attacked the soft soil, sending chrysanthemums, stocks and freesias to their deaths. He'd soon dug so deep that the hole was bigger than he was, and all that could be seen were sprays of flying soil and his fiercely wagging tail.

'Look at Buster go,' twelve-year-old Robert Edwards said, leaning on his spade. 'He could win a medal for his digging.'

Robert's best friend, Michael, laughed. 'Bark when you reach Australia!' he told Buster's rear end. He tipped the soil from his shovel on to the fast-growing mound beside them.

Buster's tail wagged as he emerged from the hole triumphant, his muddy treasure gripped firmly in his mouth.

'Oh no, better get that off him!' Robert said, when he realized what Buster had.

'What is it?' Michael asked.

'One of Dad's old slippers – he's been looking for them everywhere.'

'But how did it get down there?'

Buster cocked his head to one side, his right ear up and his left ear down.

'*Someone* must have buried it there. Buster – give!'

But Buster had no intention of giving up his treasure. As Robert moved closer to him Buster danced backwards.

'Buster – Buster – give it to me!'

Robert and Michael raced around the garden after Buster, trying to get the muddy, chewed slipper from him. Buster thought this was a wonderful new game of chase, and almost lost the slipper by barking with excitement as he dodged this way and that.

The game got even better when Robert's nine-year-old sister Lucy, and Rose the collie, came out of the house and started to chase him too.

'Buster, come back . . .'

Rose tried to circle him and cut him off. Until recently she'd been a sheepdog and she was much quicker than Buster, but he managed to evade her by jumping over the ginger-and-white cat, Tiger, who wasn't pleased to be used as a fence and hissed at Buster to tell him so.

Buster was having such a good time. First digging

up the flower bed, now playing chase. It was the perfect day – until Lucy dived on top of him and he was trapped.

'Got you!'

Robert took Dad's old slipper from Buster. 'Sorry, but you can't play with that.'

Buster jumped up at the slipper, trying to get it back. It was his – he'd buried it and he'd dug it up. Robert held the slipper above his head so Buster couldn't get it, although for such a small dog, he could jump pretty high.

Buster went back to his hole and started digging to see if he could find something else interesting. Freshly dug soil was soon flying into the air once again.

'No slacking, you two!' Robert's father, Mr Edwards, told the boys as he came out of the back door. Robert quickly hid the slipper behind him; he didn't want Buster to get into trouble. Michael took it from him, unseen.

Lucy ran back into the kitchen, with Rose close behind her.

'You two should be following Buster's example,' Mr Edwards said to the boys.

At the sound of his name Buster stopped digging for a moment and emerged from his hole. His face was covered in earth and it was clear that he was in his element. Usually he'd have been in huge trouble for digging in the garden, but not today. When

Mr Edwards wasn't looking, Michael dropped the slipper into the small ornamental fishpond near to where Tiger was lying. Tiger rubbed his head against Michael's hand, the bell on his collar tinkling softly, and Michael obligingly stroked him behind his ginger ears before getting back to work.

Tiger had been out on an early-morning prowl of the neighbourhood when the government truck had arrived and the men from it had rung the doorbell of every house along the North London terraced street. Each homeowner had been given six curved sheets of metal, two steel plates and some bolts for fixing it all together.

'There you go.'

'Shouldn't take you more than a few hours.'

'Got hundreds more of these to deliver.'

Four of the workmen helped those who couldn't manage to put up their own Anderson Shelters, but everyone else was expected to dig a large hole in their back garden, deep enough so that only two feet of the six-foot-high bomb shelter could be seen above the ground.

Buster, Robert and Michael had set to work as soon as they'd been given theirs, with Mr Edwards supervising.

'Is the hole big enough yet, Dad?' Robert asked his father. They'd been digging for ages.

Mr Edwards peered at the government instruction leaflet and shook his head. 'It needs to be four foot deep in the soil. And we'll need to dig steps down to the door.'

Tiger surveyed the goings-on through half-closed eyes from his favourite sunspot on the patio. He was content to watch as Buster wore himself out and got covered in mud. It was much too hot a day to do anything as energetic as digging.

In the kitchen, Rose was getting in the way as usual.

'Let me past, Rose,' said Lucy and Robert's mother, Mrs Edwards, turning away from the window.

Rose took a step or two backwards, but she was still in the way. The Edwardses' kitchen was small, but they'd managed to cram a wooden dresser as well as two wooden shelves and a cupboard into it. It didn't have a refrigerator.

'What were you all doing out there?' Mrs Edwards asked Lucy.

Lucy thought it best not to mention that Buster had dug up Dad's old slipper. It was from Dad's favourite pair and Mum had turned the house upside-down searching for it.

'Just playing,' she said.

Lucy began squeezing six lemon halves into a brown earthenware jug while her mother made sugar syrup by adding a cup of water and a cup of sugar to a saucepan and bringing it to the boil on the coal gas stove. Wearing a full-length apron over her button-down dress, Mrs Edwards stirred continuously so as not to scorch the syrup or the pan.

The letterbox rattled and Lucy went to see what it was. Another government leaflet lay on the mat. They seemed to be getting them almost every day now. This one had 'Sand to the Rescue' written in big letters and gave instructions on how to place sandbags so that they shielded the windows, and how to dispose of incendiary bombs using a sand-bucket and scoop.

Lucy put the leaflet on the dresser with the others and went to check on her cakes. She didn't want them to burn, especially not with Michael visiting.

Two hours later Mr Edwards declared, 'That should be enough.'

Robert and Michael stopped digging and admired their work. Buster, however, wasn't ready to stop yet. He wanted them to dig a second, even bigger hole, and he knew exactly where that hole should be. His little paws got busy digging in the new place.

'No, Buster, no more!' Robert said firmly.

Buster stopped and sat down. He watched as Robert, Michael and Mr Edwards assembled the Anderson Shelter from the six corrugated iron sheets and end plates, which they bolted together at the top.

'Right, that's it, easy does it,' Mr Edwards told the boys. The Anderson Shelter was up and in place.

For the first time Tiger became interested. The

shelter looked like a new choice sunspot – especially when the sun glinted on its corrugated iron top. He uncurled himself and sauntered over to it.

'Hello, Tiger. Come to have a look?' Michael asked him. Tiger ignored the question, jumped on to the top of the shelter and curled up on the roof.

Robert and Michael laughed. 'He must be the laziest cat in the world,' Robert said. 'All he does is eat and sleep and then sleep again.'

Tiger's sunbathing was cut short.

'You can't sleep there, Tiger,' Mr Edwards said. 'And we can't have the roof glinting in the sunshine like that. Go on – scat, cat.'

Tiger ran a few feet away and then stopped and watched as Mr Edwards and the boys now shovelled the freshly dug soil pile they'd made back on top of the roof of the bomb shelter, with Buster trying to help by digging at the pile – which wasn't really any help at all.

Mr Edwards wiped his brow as he stopped to look at the instruction leaflet again. 'It says it needs to be covered with at least fifteen inches of soil above the roof,' he told Robert and Michael.

The three of them kept on shovelling until the shelter was completely hidden by the newly dug soil.

Lucy and Mrs Edwards came out, carrying freshly made lemonade and fairy cakes.

'Good, we've earned this,' Robert said when he saw them.

'Those look very appetizing, Lucy love,' Mr Edwards said when Lucy held out the plate of cakes.

'Do you like it?' Lucy asked Michael, as he bit into his cake. Her eyes were shining.

'Delicious,' Michael smiled, and took another bite.

Buster was desperate to taste one of Lucy's cakes too. He looked at her meaningfully, mouth open, tail wagging winningly. When that didn't work he tried sitting down and lifting his paws in the air in a begging position.

Lucy furtively nudged one of the cakes off the plate on to the ground.

'Oops!'

Buster was on it and the cake was gone in one giant gulp. He looked up hopefully for more.

Mr Edwards took a long swig of his lemonade and put his beaker back on the tray. 'So, what do you think?' he asked his wife.

Mrs Edwards's flower garden was ruined. 'It's going to make it very awkward to hang out the weekly washing.'

'In a few weeks' time even I'd have trouble spotting it from the air,' Mr Edwards said. He was a reconnaissance pilot and was used to navigating from landmarks on the ground. 'It'll be covered in weeds and grass and I bet we could even grow flowers or tomato plants on it if we wanted to.'

Lucy grinned. 'But you'd still know we were nearby and wave to us from your plane, wouldn't you, Dad?'

'I would,' smiled Mr Edwards. 'With Alexandra Palace just round the corner, our street is hard to miss. But Jerry flying over with his bombs won't have a clue the Anderson Shelter's down here with you hidden inside it – and that's the main thing.'

Lucy shivered. 'Will there really be another war, Dad?' It was a question everyone was asking.

'I hope not. I really do,' Mr Edwards said, putting his arm round his wife. 'They called the last one the Great War and told us it was the war to end all wars. But now that looks doubtful.'

Michael helped himself to another of Lucy's cakes and smiled at her.

Lucy was beaming as she went back inside, with Rose following her.

As Lucy filled Buster's bowl with fresh water and took it back outside, Rose padded behind her like a shadow. She chose different people, and occasionally Buster or Tiger, to follow on different days. But she chose Lucy most of all. She'd tried to herd Buster and Tiger once or twice, as she used to do with the sheep, but so far this hadn't been very successful, due to Buster and Tiger's lack of cooperation.

'Here, Buster, you must be thirsty too after all that digging,' Lucy said, putting his water bowl down on the patio close to Tiger, who stretched out his legs and flexed his sharp claws. Lucy stroked him and Tiger purred.

Buster lapped at the water with his little pink tongue.

'Buster deserves a bone for all that digging,' Robert said. 'Or at least a biscuit or two.'

Buster looked up at him and wagged his tail.

'Go on then,' Mrs Edwards said.

Robert went inside and came back with Buster's tin of dog biscuits. Buster wagged his tail even more enthusiastically at the sight of the tin, and wolfed down the biscuit Robert gave him. Bones or biscuits – food was food.

'Here, Rose, want a biscuit?' Robert asked her.

Rose accepted one and then went to lie down beside the bench on which Lucy was sitting. She preferred it when everyone was together in the same place; only then could she really settle.

Just a few months ago Rose had been living in Devon and working as a sheepdog. But things had changed when the elderly farmer didn't come out one morning, or the next. Rose waited for the farmer at the back door from dawn to dusk and then went back to the barn where she slept. But the farmer never came.

Some days the farmer's wife brought a plate of food for her. Some days she forgot and Rose went to sleep hungry.

Then the farmer's daughter, Mrs Edwards, came to the farm, dressed in black, and the next day she took Rose back to London with her on the train. Rose never saw the farmer again.

Rose whined and Lucy bent and stroked her head.

'Feeling sad?' she asked her.

Sometimes Rose had a faraway look in her eyes that made Lucy wonder just what Rose was thinking. Did she miss Devon? It must be strange for Rose only having a small garden to run about in when she was used to herding sheep with her grandfather on the moor.

'Do you miss Grandad?'

Rose licked Lucy's hand.

'I miss him too,' Lucy said.

When they all went back indoors, Tiger stayed in the garden. He took a step closer to the Anderson Shelter and then another step and another. Tiger was a very curious sort of cat, and being shooed away had only made him more curious. He ran down the earth steps and peered into the new construction.

Inside it was dark, but felt cool and slightly damp after the heat of the sun.

'Tiger!' Lucy called, coming back out. 'Tiger, where are you?'

Lucy came down the garden and found him.

'There you are. Why didn't you come when I called you?' She picked Tiger up like a baby, with his paws waving in the air, and carried him out of the shelter and back up to the house. It wasn't the most comfortable or dignified way of travelling, but Tiger put up with it because it was Lucy. Ever since Tiger had arrived at the Edwardses' house as a tiny mewling kitten, he and Lucy had had a special bond.

They stopped at the living room where Robert was showing Michael Buster's latest trick.

'Slippers, Buster,' Robert said.

Buster raced to the shoe rack by the front door, found Robert's blue leather slippers and raced back with one of them in his mouth. He dropped the slipper beside Robert.

Robert put his foot in it and said, 'Slippers,' again. Buster raced off and came back with the other one.

Robert gave him a dog biscuit.

Michael grinned. 'He's so smart.'

'He can identify Dad and Mum and Lucy's slippers too,' Robert told Michael. He'd decided not to risk Dad's new slippers with Buster today. 'You're one clever dog, aren't you, Buster?'

Buster wagged his tail like mad and then raced round and round, chasing it.

'Tiger and Rose can do tricks too,' Lucy said, putting Tiger down in an armchair. 'And Rose doesn't need to be bribed with food to do them. Look – down, Rose.'

Rose obediently lay down.

Lucy moved across the room and Rose started to stand up to follow her.

'Stay, Rose.'

Rose lay back down again.

'Good girl.'

'So what tricks can Tiger do?' Michael asked Lucy.

Lucy pulled a strand of wool from her mum's knitting basket and waggled it in front of Tiger like a snake wriggling around the carpet. Tiger jumped off the armchair, stalked the wool and captured it with his paw.

Tail held high, he went over to Robert and then to Michael to allow them the honour of stroking him.

Tiger didn't need tricks to be admired.

Chapter 2

Since the spring of 1939 every school in the country had been prepared for the possibility of war. Millions of gas masks had been given out to both adults and children, and everyone had to carry them at all times. Gas masks had even been made for dogs and horses. Buster and Rose didn't have gas masks yet, and goodness knows how they would react if they were forced to wear them.

None had been made for cats because no one was foolish enough to believe that a cat would wear a gas mask. Getting Tiger to wear one would have been just about impossible! You'd get scratched to pieces trying to put it on him – that's if you were able to catch him in the first place.

Lucy hated the gas mask she'd been given at school. The grown-ups called them Mickey Mouse masks to try and make the lurid pink monstrosities seem less sinister. But the masks didn't look anything like Mickey Mouse, or any other sort of mouse.

Lucy knew the mask could save her life if there was a gas attack, but she still loathed it. Just the thought of wearing it made her feel sick, and once she had it on she felt suffocated because there wasn't enough air coming through the filter to breathe easily and all she could smell was rubber.

Even worse, her class had to have a gas-mask drill twice a week. They'd all been given Ministry of Safety leaflets, which explained how to put the masks on:

1. Hold your breath.
2. Hold your mask in front of your face with your thumbs inside the straps.
3. Thrust your chin well forward into the mask and pull the straps over your head as far as they will go.
4. Run your fingers round the face part of the mask to make sure the head straps are not twisted.

Miss Morrison blew a whistle. 'Gas-mask practice,' she announced. 'Take your gas masks out of their boxes.'

Miss Morrison always wore a whistle round her neck now so that if there was a war and she got buried by rubble, people would be able to find her.

'I want you to put your gas masks on with your eyes closed today. A gas attack might come at any time – day or night.'

'Can't see out of the bloomin' thing anyway,' grumbled a boy behind Lucy, who'd already put his gas mask on.

And he was right. Lucy always found that just about as soon as she put her mask on, the Perspex misted up. Rubbing soap on the window, which they'd been told would help, made it worse and you got soap in your eyes too. There was only one thing the masks were really good for.

'On the count of three . . .' Miss Morrison said. And everyone picked up their masks, ready to put on the much-hated things.

'One . . . two . . . . three!'

Lucy blew out through the rubber instead of in, to make a long, loud fart sound.

Miss Morrison was furious.

'Who did that? Who was it? Who did it?'

She stared at a sea of children in gas masks. It was impossible to tell who'd made the sound.

Other children blew out too and Miss Morrison looked as though she was going to explode.

Behind her mask Lucy grinned, until Miss Morrison announced that she was keeping the whole class in at breaktime as punishment for their 'disgraceful behaviour'.

Robert and Michael were two of the very few children at their school who weren't going to be evacuated with the rest of their classmates. Robert was going to stay with his gran in Devon and Michael wasn't going to be evacuated at all. He was staying in London with his family.

Michael's father was an Animal Guard and had been issued with a NARPAC – National Air Raid Precautions Animals Committee – registration book to write down the names and addresses of all animals that were reported lost or missing during air raids, should the war come. He also had an armband and a tin hat with NARPAC written on it.

'So what else will your dad be doing if there's a war?' Robert asked Michael over their fish-pie school dinner.

'Patrolling the local area and helping any animals that have been injured in the air raids. And taking injured animals and strays to the rescue centre. I'm going to help him.'

One day, if he passed enough exams, Michael hoped to be a vet.

Robert was fascinated by Michael's dad's work as an Animal Guard and now a NARPAC volunteer; he wished he could be doing something useful to help with the war effort too. But the other kids in Michael's class made fun of him for it.

'You smell like a dog, Michael,' a boy in the next row of desks said.

Michael didn't care. He liked the smell of dogs.

'Your parents are crazy for letting you stay in

London, Michael,' some kids at the next table said. 'Don't they read the posters?'

There were posters everywhere telling parents it was better for their children to be moved out of London and away from the risk of bombs to the safety of the countryside. One showed Hitler whispering to an unsuspecting mother that she was wrong to send her children away. 'You're doing what Hitler wants by letting them stay,' read the caption.

'You're playing right into Jerry's hands, Michael,' said Mark Talbot. Everyone had started calling the Germans Jerries.

'Don't let them get to you,' Robert told Michael. Michael just shrugged. 'I won't.'

Most people in the class were looking forward to being evacuated and saw it as a great adventure. They didn't think it would last long. 'It'll just be for a few weeks and then Hitler will surrender and the Jerries will go crying back to their mums and we'll come home victorious,' Mark Talbot said.

'Few weeks' free holiday,' grinned Dick Holmes.

'My mum says I'm to make the most of it,' said Emily Clarke.

'Shame Sloggings has got to come though,' everyone agreed.

Mr Sloggart was their form teacher. He was a short bald man who always wore a mortar board hat and gown, and had round-rimmed glasses. His face went very red when he got in a temper. Robert tried not to be one of the ones who riled him because Mr Sloggart could be pretty free with the cane on your hand or backside if you got on the wrong side of him.

'Bet you wish you were coming with the rest of us,' Dick said to Robert.

'It looks like it's going to be fun,' Robert said. But he was more envious of Michael being allowed to stay in London and help with the war effort than of those who were being evacuated with the school. He wished he could stay too. But all those parents who had relatives in the countryside who could look after their children had been advised to send them there.

Mrs Edwards had been worried about it at first.

'Make sure you and Lucy are no trouble to your gran, and help out as much as you can. She's very frail and hasn't been finding it at all easy since your grandfather passed away.'

Robert and Lucy both promised that they'd be no trouble at all.

There was a letter from their gran waiting for Robert when he got home from school that day. He took it up to his room where he found Tiger curled up on his bed. Robert shifted him over a bit to make some room.

'What's it say?' Lucy asked, coming to stand in

the doorway, with Rose behind her. Gran hadn't written a letter to Lucy.

Robert tore the envelope open.

My dearest Bertie,
I hope you are well and have the warm socks I made you.
I heard that the trenches can get terribly cold. The chicken
with the damaged wing laid three speckled eggs this week.
I'm so looking forward to Robert and Lucy's visit and
have made some cakes for them. If only the Great War
was over and you could come home. I do miss you . . .

'It doesn't make much sense,' Robert said, as he handed Lucy the letter to read.

'Who's Bertie?'

'Uncle Bertie – Mum's older brother. He died before we were born.'

'So the letter wasn't really to you?'

'She sent it here.'

Lucy frowned. 'Gran's not really OK, is she?'

'We'll manage.'

'But will she be able to look after us?'

'Course. And anyway, we can look after ourselves.'

Lucy nodded. No need to show the letter to Mum. She'd only worry.

Chapter 3

Tension filled the air as Robert and Lucy sat on the floor by the wireless waiting to hear the prime minister, Mr Chamberlain, address the nation. Robert watched his mother squeeze his father's hand.

'Does it really have to come to this?' she said softly.

Two days ago, on September the first, Germany had invaded Poland. Yesterday Mr Chamberlain had issued an ultimatum to say that if the German troops were not withdrawn, then war would be declared. Everyone had known that Britain could be forced to declare war to stop Hitler's attempted takeover of Europe, but no one wanted another world war. Many people's memories were still full of horrific recollections of the first one.

Robert thought Britain would be right if it went to war. Mr Hitler was a bully and Britain couldn't let the bullies win. Sometimes he found himself wishing he was old enough to go and fight. But he never said so because he knew his mother's elder brother – who he was named after – had died during the Great War. He felt a bit guilty for not telling his parents about Gran's odd letter, but they already had so much to worry about. They didn't need him adding to it. This wasn't like a fight at school; people, possibly millions of people, were going to be killed.

At precisely 11.15 Mr Chamberlain started to speak. His voice was sombre.

'I am speaking to you from the Cabinet Room at 10 Downing Street. This morning the British ambassador in Berlin handed the German government a final note stating that unless we heard from them by 11.00 a.m. that they were prepared at once to withdraw their troops from Poland, a state of war would exist between us.

'I have to tell you that no such undertaking has been received, and that consequently this country is at war with Germany.'

Lucy gasped and put her hand to her mouth. A tear rolled down Mrs Edwards's face. The news she'd been dreading had come.

Mr Chamberlain continued: 'Up to the very last it would have been quite possible to have arranged a peaceful and honourable settlement between Germany and Poland, but Hitler would not have it.'

Buster rolled over so his head was resting on Rose. She didn't seem to mind.

'His actions show convincingly that there is no chance of expecting that this man will ever give up his practice of using force to gain his will. He can only be stopped by force.'

Robert looked at Mr Edwards's clenched fist. Mrs Edwards and Lucy looked shocked and bewildered. Only the pets seemed to be at peace. At least they had no idea of what was to come. Tiger was curled up in Mum's lap, Rose was dozing on the rug in front of the unlit fire with Buster lying with his head resting on her back.

'You may be taking part in the fighting services or as a volunteer in one of the branches of civil defence. If so, you will report for duty in accordance with the instructions you have received.

'You may be engaged in work essential to the prosecution of war for the maintenance of the life of the people – in factories, in transport, in public utility concerns or in the supply of other necessaries of life. If so, it is of vital importance that you should carry on with your jobs.

'Now may God bless you all. May He defend the right. It is the evil things that we shall be fighting against – brute force, bad faith, injustice, oppression and persecution – and against them I am certain that the right will prevail.'

At the end of Mr Chamberlain's devastating news the air-raid sirens sounded and even the pets' peace was shattered. It was an eerie wailing sound like a banshee heralding death.

Tiger leapt off Mrs Edwards's lap and raced away

up the stairs to Lucy's bed. Rose growled and then started to bark, and Buster ran to Robert for reassurance.

'It's all right, Buster,' Robert said as he stroked the little dog and the sound of the air-raid siren faded away. But he knew that it wasn't all right. Not all right at all, really.

Mr Edwards pulled on his coat. 'I need to get back to the airbase,' he said.

Mrs Edwards ran upstairs to fetch his suitcase, which was already packed with his pilot's uniform as he'd been due to leave in the morning. Now it seemed there was no time to waste.

'I don't want you to go,' Lucy said.

Mr Edwards hugged her to him. 'I have to, poppet,' he told her. 'We can't let Mr Hitler win, can we?'

Lucy shook her head.

Mr Edwards shook Robert's hand. 'Take good care of them,' he said.

'I will,' Robert told him. 'I won't let anything bad happen.'

'Good lad. And you be good,' he told Lucy.

'I will,' she promised.

Buster looked up at Mr Edwards and wagged his tail.

'You be good too,' Mr Edwards told him, as he patted the little dog.

Mrs Edwards handed him his suitcase and he

kissed her. Then he pulled the front door open and hurried down the path before they could see the tears in his eyes.

Rose watched him go from the doorway. Tiger watched him from Lucy's bedroom window ledge.

Buster whined and Mrs Edwards looked down. He had one of Mr Edwards's new slippers in his mouth.

When Mr Edwards arrived back at the airfield that evening, he was greeted by the voice of Adolf Hitler on the wireless. 'Britain need expect nothing other than annihilation as an enemy of the nation of Germany.'

'Sad day,' the wing commander said.

Mr Edwards couldn't agree more. It was indeed a very sad day. He put his suitcase on his bed to unpack later and went over to the pigeon loft. His old friend Jim, the pigeon wrangler with the long moustache, handed him a cup of tea in a tin mug. He was just about to feed the birds.

'There'll need to be more reconnaissance flights now.'

Mr Edwards nodded and took a swig of his tea. Jim's tea was so strong people joked that the teaspoon stood up by itself in it.

'More danger to your lot and the WAAFs.'

Mr Edwards nodded again.

The Women's Auxiliary Air Force weren't actually

allowed to be involved with combat flights as it was felt that life-givers shouldn't also be life-takers. But they flew the planes from one airfield to another and were part of the ground crew. Their roles included aircraft detection, code-breaking and, most importantly to Mr Edwards, analysis of the reconnaissance photographs that his crew took.

Many pilots wanted to be fighters in the war, but Mr Edwards knew that the photo reconnaissance missions he was involved in were often more important and more productive than the bombing missions. Information was needed both before attacking the enemy and afterwards to see what had been achieved.

Jim's pigeons too had an important role to play. They could mean the difference between an SOS message getting through and the crew from a plane that had been hit being rescued – or not.

Once a homing pigeon understood that their home was their home, they knew with some amazing instinct how to get back to it, from anywhere. And as the airfield was now their home, to the airfield they would always return, bringing their vital message, written on a tiny piece of tissue paper in the carrier that was attached to their leg.

'See you've got some eggs,' Mr Edwards said.

'Yup,' Jim said, twirling his moustache. 'Should hatch in another day or two.'

These eggs had come from two of his best homing birds and he had high hopes for the hatchlings that came from them. Training the squabs would start even before the young birds had taken their first flight.

Jim would put food and water in the pigeon loft so the young pigeons would know that was where they were fed. This needed to be done for a minimum of two weeks. Once the two weeks were up, he'd let the birds out for the first time.

Some of them would fly around crazily. Some of them would flutter about a little and then walk about on the ground instead. But when they were hungry they'd return to the loft to eat.

Gradually, Jim would increase the distance he took the birds before releasing them and letting them return to the loft, until he was five and then ten and then even fifty miles away.

The older birds who'd reached the fifty-mile stage still needed to practise regularly, and Jim would drive off with them once a week and release them from different points and places so they could find their way home from any direction.

'The first few weeks are the hardest. More than one of them has caused me to want to pull my hair out and wonder if they had any homing instinct at all. But once it kicks in and the birds start flying home, it's pretty wonderful to see.'

Mr Edwards smiled and put his empty tin mug down.

'See you in the morning.'

'I'll have two of my best waiting for you.'

Flight Lieutenant William Edwards was one of the favoured few who was welcome at the pigeon loft. Jim was very strict about who went near it because more than anything the pigeons needed to feel safe there and want to return home when they were released. 'If you scare the birds by poking your fingers into their loft, then they won't want to come home, will they? And some poor bloke might be dead because of it,' he'd say to anyone foolish enough to do so.

Mr Edwards headed over to the aircraft hangar. He was the pilot of a Blenheim plane that he'd christened Buster. The Blenheims had only been around for a few years and previously he'd flown a biplane that had been much slower. His Blenheim could reach 260mph.

It was constructed of all-metal materials with the wings positioned midway up the fuselage and, unlike his old biplane, it had retractable landing gear and flaps.

Buster was a creation of beauty in Mr Edwards's opinion – although hard to handle, and freezing cold. It had a crew of four, and all the airmen had thick, fleecy coats to wear.

'She's all ready to go, sir,' the engineer called out to him from the cockpit window.

Mr Edwards put his thumbs up.

There was not a lot of room for the pilot in the Blenheim and the tips of the propellers were only a foot or so away from the cockpit side windows.

It was so cramped that when he sat in his place, on the left side of the plane's nose, he couldn't even see some of the instruments. The propeller pitch control was behind him and had to be operated by touch alone.

Cramped or not, he loved his plane. But that evening he looked at it and worried. It was better at night flights, but during the day, out on a reconnaissance sortie, would it really stand a chance against a German Messerschmitt?

Chapter 4

The total black-out from 1 September onwards meant that no house lights, car headlights or street lights were allowed to be seen. This did not put Tiger or his cat friends off their night-time prowl. Tiger arrived home at a little before dawn, just as Mr Edwards was setting off on a flight to France.

Tiger caught up on his sleep on Lucy's pillow while Robert and Lucy took Rose and Buster for one last walk on the morning that they were being evacuated down to Devon.

'I'm going to miss them so much,' Lucy said as they headed down the road to the park. She swallowed hard to try to get rid of the lump in her throat.

'Me too,' said Robert. 'But with any luck the war will be over in a few weeks' time and we'll all be back together.'

Lucy had heard the 'short war' rumour too, but she was doubtful that it could be over so quickly.

As soon as he saw they were heading for the park, Buster started pulling on his lead.

Why were they going so slowly? Didn't they real-ize that the quicker they went the sooner they'd get there?

He strained on his lead, making wheezing sounds.

'Take it easy, Buster. You don't want to choke your-self,' Robert told him.

Buster tried to slow down, but after a few seconds he'd forgotten and started pulling on his lead again.

Lucy was having a much easier time with Rose. Even though Rose had hardly ever had occasion to walk on a lead when she'd lived on the farm down in Devon, she'd quickly grasped the concept of walk-ing at Lucy's side rather than ahead of her.

'Good girl, Rose,' Lucy told her.

Once they'd gone through the park gate, they let the dogs off their leads. Buster was so excited that he raced around as fast as his short legs would go – which was pretty fast.

Rose padded along beside Lucy and Robert at first, but even she wasn't immune to the excitement of the park, with its intriguing smells and other dogs to play with. She raced after Buster and they ran together, almost dancing, across the grass.

Robert and Lucy stopped to say hello to a yellow Labrador puppy, and Buster and Rose came running back to see what was going on.

'He's so sweet,' Lucy said as she stroked the puppy.

'His name's Toby and let me tell you he can be quite a handful,' the woman who was with him told them. 'He's my daughter's dog, but I'm the one who has to clear up all the mess he makes.'

Toby rolled over on to his back and Buster gave him a sniff before letting the puppy clamber all over him.

'Toby, come on – you'll be the death of me, you will,' the woman said. She clipped Toby's lead to his collar and dragged him away. Toby looked back at Rose and Buster. Playtime had been much too short.

Robert and Lucy carried on walking with Buster and Rose, who stopped every now and again to sniff interesting smells before racing to catch up with the children.

They came to the large lake that had ducks swimming on it.

Robert clipped Buster's lead back on.

'Just in case,' Robert said to Lucy, with a meaningful look. 'We don't want to have to be fishing him out of there – today of all days.'

Lucy took a deep breath. Momentarily she'd forgotten this was their last walk with Buster and Rose. She was determined not to cry because it would only upset the dogs, especially Rose who was very sensitive.

As soon as they got home, Lucy ran up the stairs to find Tiger, and buried her face in his soft fur. Tiger rubbed his head against Lucy's and purred.

Downstairs Robert rolled around on the floor with Buster, the last wrestling match they'd have for a long time. Buster made the most of it by jumping all over him and licking his ear.

Upstairs, Lucy picked up the small brown cardboard suitcase that was lying on the bed beside her gas mask and identity card. Inside it she had a change of clothes, a toothbrush, a sketchbook and some pencils. You were only allowed to take as much as you could carry by yourself so Lucy had packed carefully.

'Time to go!' Mrs Edwards called up the stairs, dashing a tear away before the children saw. It broke her heart to let Robert and Lucy go, but she really didn't have any other choice. She was going to be based on a special floating hospital on the River Thames during the war, and of course her husband was already back at the airbase continuing his reconnaissance work.

Lucy hugged Rose at the front door. 'Goodbye, good girl,' she said, and kissed Rose on the top of her furry head.

After Mrs Edwards and the children had left, Rose stood for a long while staring at the door through which they'd gone out. Buster looked at Rose and then looked at the door and whined. Tiger headed upstairs for more sleep.

When they arrived at Paddington Station, Mrs Edwards looked around her in dismay. There were hordes and hordes of people there. They'd have to push their way through to the platform.

'Make sure you stay close,' Mrs Edwards said to Robert. It would be easy for them to get separated in the throng. She took Lucy's hand. Their train was at platform 12. It wouldn't take them all the way to Witherton on the Moor, where their grandmother lived, but Mrs Edwards had been assured that buses would be provided to take the evacuated children to the outlying villages.

Whole schools were travelling together and there was an air of jubilation – as if they were off on a free school outing.

Mrs Edwards spoke to a teacher whose school was going down to Newton Abbot. When she explained their situation, she was told not to worry – they would take care of Robert and Lucy.

'Some of the children on the train are going to be billeted at Witherton on the Moor and they'll be attending the village school with your two.'

It was time to board.

'Two by two,' the teacher shouted. 'Orderly fashion.'

Lucy noted that this school had been practising the evacuation process, just as hers had done.

Mrs Edwards hugged Robert and Lucy to her.

'I'm worried about Tiger. What if he goes out at night and can't find Mrs Harris's house?' Lucy said.

'He'll be fine,' Mrs Edwards reassured her.

Mrs Edwards was sure of that. Elsie Harris was an ex-nursing colleague of hers, and very reliable.

The pets would be safe and well looked-after with her.

The whistle blew.

'Bye, Mum.'

'See you soon.'

Mrs Edwards hoped she *would* see them soon, hoped it more than anything in the world. She tried to wave to them both through the windows, but she couldn't see where they'd sat and the children all seemed to have their faces pressed against the glass and none of the faces were Lucy's or Robert's.

The whistle blew again and the train pulled out and away, leaving Mrs Edwards standing helplessly on the platform.

She left the station and caught the crowded bus back home. There were many other mothers on board the bus, looking shocked, with their handkerchiefs pressed to their faces to stem the tears. Like Mrs Edwards, they'd had to say goodbye to their children.

Mrs Edwards steeled herself not to cry. Most of her fellow mothers on the bus didn't know who their children were going to. A lot of them didn't even know exactly where they were going. At least her two weren't going to strangers – they'd be staying with her mother in a place they knew. Although she'd never really been close to her mother since her elder brother's death in the Great War, she knew she would take good care of them.

Mrs Edwards looked at her watch. She was going to have to hurry to get the pets over to the Harrises' house before she was due to report at the floating hospital.

Chapter 5

Some cats take time to adjust to a new home and
new people. Cats that are moved only a short distance
of a few miles or so, often return to their old home
and many need to be kept indoors for the first two
or three weeks.

Tiger wasn't like those cats.

As soon as they were left at the Harrises' house, the
ginger-and-white cat found the most comfortable
chair and claimed it as his own by circling it twice – to
press out any lumps and bumps in the cushions – and
then settling down and closing his eyes.

While Rose lay awake most of the night and
Buster whimpered in his sleep, Tiger slept soundly.
He stayed in his chosen chair and on their first morning, apart from the odd toilet break, that's where he
was to be found. The chair was next to the wireless
in the faded flock-wallpapered living room. The
room was dark and yellowed by coal and tobacco-
smoke stains, the greying net curtains at the windows
doing little to help brighten the place.

Rose lay by the hearth in the same room as Tiger, close to his chair. A beige rug that had seen better days protected her a little from the cold of the stone floor. She stared into the space where the unlit fire's flames should be.

At least Buster was warm. He was in the kitchen with Mrs Harris, hoping for any scraps. Anything at all would do, he wasn't particular, but he was always hungry. The Harrises' house smelt of cooked cabbage. Buster would have willingly given cabbage a try if Mrs Harris would just give him some.

'Get out of the way, Buster,' Mrs Harris said. She was trying to get ready to go out and, wherever she went, there he was at her feet. 'You'll have me over at this rate.'

Both Mrs Harris and Buster turned at the sound of slippered footsteps on the stairs. Mr Harris was on his way. He coughed, a morning phlegm-clearing ritual that he never missed.

'Cup of tea, dear,' Mrs Harris called out cheerily.

Mr Harris gave a muttered response that Mrs Harris took to mean *Yes, please, dearest, a cup of tea would be lovely.*

'Will you get out of the way,' she told Buster once again. His tail wagged. She was weakening. His persistence finally worked and she threw him a crust of bread. He wolfed it down in one gulp and then looked at her hopefully for more.

'That's it. No more!' Mrs Harris said.

Mr Harris didn't come into the kitchen. He picked up the newspaper from the hallway and went straight into the living room. He was wearing yesterday's vest and dark striped trousers with braces, one of which was on his shoulder and the other round his waist.

Mr Harris was about to sit down when he saw Tiger. Tiger miaowed winningly, but Mr Harris wasn't pleased to find a cat in his chair and swiped Tiger on the nose with his rolled-up newspaper. Tiger gave a howl of surprise and protest, and then, seeing Mr Harris was about to hit him again, jumped nimbly off the chair.

'Is everything all right in there?' Mrs Harris called from the kitchen.

'Everything's fine,' came the reply.

'What's wrong with that cat?'

'How am I supposed to know? Dumb animal.'

Rose looked at Mr Harris with her unusual blue eyes. He stared back at her, and she sighed and turned her head away.

Mr Harris sat down in his chair and opened his newspaper with a flourish.

Tiger tried to jump on Mr Harris's lap, damaging the newspaper.

'Gerroff!'

Tiger had to settle for the back of the armchair and a view of the pink bald patch on top of Mr Harris's head.

Mr Harris scowled as he smoothed out his crumpled

newspaper. He thought it was an imposition of the Edwardses to ask them to look after their animals. He'd never been all that keen on Mrs Edwards, who he'd once caught looking disapprovingly down her nose at him. She had no call to consider herself above him. He, in his opinion, was just as good as the likes of her.

'And don't she forget it,' he said, not realizing his last phrase had been said aloud.

'What did you say, dear?' Mrs Harris asked, breezing in with his cup of tea.

He noted that the Jack Russell, constantly at her heels ever since the animals had arrived, was with her.

Mr Harris scowled at his wife. She was always breezing about these days. Busy as a buzzing bee, when what she should have been doing was taking care of him.

'It's not like they're paying us to look after them,' he said, nodding at the animals.

Mrs Harris breezed out again, having decided for one reason or another not to mention the money that had changed hands between Mrs Edwards and herself. She took off her apron.

'There's porridge for you on the stove. Give them a bit of whatever's left over, would you?'

Mr Harris didn't reply. He shouldn't be expected to get his own breakfast or give it to the mutts they had staying with them. He knocked the remnants of tobacco from his pipe into the ashtray.

Mrs Harris buttoned up her coat. 'Bye, love,' she called from the front door. 'I've got an extra shift so I won't be back till late tonight.'

'Hrumph.'

When she'd gone, Mr Harris stood up with a groan and went to the kitchen. He helped himself to a large bowl of porridge and sprinkled it with three heaped tablespoons of sugar before sitting down at the small Formica-topped table to eat it.

Buster sat on the floor by Mr Harris's feet. He looked up at him with his head tilted to one side, pleading for a spoonful or two of porridge. Mr Harris studiously ignored him. He prided himself on not being a soft touch.

He didn't give the animals porridge. He didn't give them anything at all. He scraped up every last mouthful of porridge himself and left his bowl on the table.

Buster followed Mr Harris as he went back into the living room, watching as he pushed Tiger out of his chair once again and sat down.

'Dumb animals.'

Mr Harris picked up his unlit pipe and sucked on it thoughtfully as he looked at Rose, Buster and Tiger. He hadn't asked to have any of them billeted with them. He should have been consulted.

There'd been talk about what should happen to pets, what with the war now coming, in the pub last night, and mention of a place nearby where they could be seen to.

Tiger jumped into the armchair as soon as Mr Harris left the room.

When he came back half an hour later, Mr Harris was washed and had a shirt and knitted bottle-green waistcoat over his vest. He left his slippers by the unlit fire and laced up his outdoor shoes.

Buster wagged his tail. But it wasn't just Buster, it transpired, who was going out.

Children were squashed three and four to a seat on the bus that bumped down the country lanes towards Witherton on the Moor. There was nowhere to put the one suitcase of clothes or the single toy that each child was allowed to bring with them, so children had them balanced awkwardly on their laps or in the way at their feet. On the train some of them had had to use their suitcases as seats.

'I feel sick,' five-year-old Charlie complained to Lucy.

'Try your hardest not to be,' she told him. Although the truth was she was feeling sick too. The road twisted and turned so, and she longed for the journey to be over. The pets wouldn't have liked the long train ride or this trip on the bus either, but she still wished, more than anything, that she and Robert could have brought Tiger, Buster and Rose with them.

'Look!' someone cried out, and pointed.

Children's noses pressed to the bus windows. To

the right of them the sea sparkled. For most of the children it was the first time they'd seen it.

'It's so huge.'

'Them waves look dangerous.'

Robert smiled. The sea wasn't dangerous. Not if you knew how to swim like he did. He'd been in and out of the sea two years ago when they'd come here to visit his grandparents.

'You're like a little seal,' his grandfather had commented proudly as he'd ruffled Robert's wet hair. 'Just like I used to be.'

That was when he was ten and Lucy was seven and it was the last time he'd seen his grandfather. There'd been a letter, just before Easter, telling them Grandad was now in heaven. His mother had gone to the funeral and come back with Rose.

If they were close to the sea, then they must be coming close to Witherton on the Moor. Half an hour later the journey was over. The children piled out of the bus, looking slightly dazed. Many of them had been up since the early hours of the morning, waiting at Paddington. It had been a very long day and it wasn't over yet.

'This way,' Miss Hubbard shouted, pointing towards the chapel. Miss Hubbard was a tall, thin woman of about thirty, with short, curled brunette hair. She'd been the one in charge of their carriage on the long train trip from London, and she was just about worn out.

Robert heard the local people muttering as they filed past them, holding their suitcases, in a crocodile line towards the chapel.

'Too many of them . . .'

'Never have enough lice powder . . .'

'. . . extra mouths to feed.'

And worse: 'They should be sent back to where they came from.'

Little Charlie, whose hand Lucy insisted on holding, looked like he was about to start snivelling at any second. Robert wished Lucy would let go of him. He wasn't their responsibility. Charlie would have to take care of himself. But of course Lucy didn't see it like that. She'd always been a soft touch. Buster could wrap her round any of his paws, and would be as fat as a pig if Lucy was left in charge of him all the time.

Lucy looked over at Robert and smiled. He knew what that smile meant. It was her *Can we keep him?* smile. She'd really taken Charlie under her wing. When she got a bee in her bonnet, it was easier to go along with her rather than go against what she wanted to do. Lucy, for all her kindness, could be the most stubborn person in the world when she thought it was for a good cause.

His father's words rang in Robert's ears. 'You're the oldest, I'm depending on you to take care of her.' Robert wouldn't let him down.

'Hurry up, now. No dawdling,' Miss Hubbard said

as they went through the chapel door. The chapel smelt damp and dusty. Villagers sat, unsmiling, in the pews. Miss Hubbard ushered everyone in. The headmaster of the evacuees' school, Mr Faber, was having a cup of tea and a slice of cake with the vicar.

'That's it, Charlie,' Robert said encouragingly.

Charlie, if anything, looked even more miserable than before. He certainly felt it.

The problem was that Charlie really, *really* needed to go to the toilet. He'd tried to ask Miss Hubbard, but he was small and not very brave and she was too busy to notice him.

'Quickly – line up. Smallest at the front. Boys and girls separate. You,' she pointed at Charlie.

Charlie pointed to himself. 'Me?' he mouthed silently, and let go of Lucy's hand. Maybe Miss Hubbard had realized he needed to go to the toilet. Maybe he had a look about him that said *I can't last one minute longer*. He wished for at least the millionth time that day that he'd been able to go when his mother had told him to at home. He wished he hadn't lied to her and said that he'd been when he hadn't.

Miss Hubbard grabbed Charlie by the arm – hard enough to hurt – and pulled him away from Lucy to stand in the front row.

'No one will be able to see you hidden back there, will they, you silly boy?'

The girl who'd been standing on the other side of

Charlie sidled over to Lucy. It was the girl with the dirty fingernails, who'd pinched her and then claimed she hadn't, on the train.

'Not got your big brother to protect you now, have you?' she said.

Lucy edged away from her, but there was really nowhere for her to go. The chapel was barely big enough to hold them all. She was in the second row of children, as she was neither tall nor small but in the middle, and from where she was standing she could see Charlie clearly. She wondered why on earth he was standing in such a peculiar way with his legs so tightly crossed. She frowned. It was almost as if . . . as if . . .

Charlie couldn't hold on any longer. He had to go. Tears streamed down his face as the urine soaked through his short trousers and down his bare leg.

Lucy bit her lip. What she'd dreaded happening had happened.

All the villagers saw. She could see the distaste on their faces.

'Well, what else would you expect from a child like that?'

'No manners.'

'No self-control.'

She felt angry on Charlie's behalf. She wanted to go to him and tell him it'd be all right, but Miss Hubbard had already grabbed him and pulled him away.

'You naughty boy,' Miss Hubbard said, shaking him roughly. 'Why didn't you tell me you needed to use the toilet?'

Charlie opened and closed his mouth, but couldn't seem to be able to say any words. Snot trickled down his face.

'Oh for heaven's sake, wipe your nose and then go and change your clothes.' She pointed to where the toilet was.

Charlie didn't have a handkerchief so he did the only thing he could think of and wiped it on his sleeve.

Chapter 6

The Wood Green Animal Shelter had been set up
to rescue animals after the Great War. The short
journey from the Harrises' North London house to
the shelter had not been easy, due to Mr Harris reck-
oning he could sell Tiger's cat basket and so deciding
to carry Tiger instead.

Tiger turned out to be a wriggler and the two dogs
hadn't made it any easier. Rose went too slowly and
kept stopping while Buster spent his time trying to
choke himself on his lead by racing ahead.

Worse, when he got there, Mr Harris found he
wasn't the only one. There must have been more
than a hundred people with pets in the queue in
front of him. Maybe even two hundred.

'It'll break my little girl's heart when she finds out
what I've done,' said a woman with a yellow Labrador puppy that kept trying to play with Buster. 'Stop
it, Toby – leave him alone.'

The puppy whined.

'Needs must. There's a war coming. No time for

sentimentality,' said someone else with two spaniels that Rose and Buster were sniffing at, all four of their tails wagging happily in greeting.

'A dog would eat you as soon as kill you when they're hungry,' said a fat man with a miniature poodle.

'We've got to think of the baby. Can't trust the dog with it,' a lank-haired woman said, while her whippet looked up at her adoringly.

'And they spread diseases,' said a fox-fur-coated woman with a Siamese cat. The cat hissed at Tiger and Tiger arched his back and hissed in reply, almost escaping from Mr Harris's arms as he did so.

'No you don't!' Mr Harris clamped the pesky cat to his chest. Tiger gave him a look of utter disgust, but there wasn't anything he could do. He was effectively trapped. Mr Harris had his right arm firmly round Tiger and was holding both of the dogs' leads with his left.

As he listened to the people around him, Mr Harris started to think that bringing the animals to the shelter to be put down was more effort than it was worth. He could be stuck in this queue for over an hour, maybe even two.

'Rabid dogs could bring this country to its knees faster than Mr Hitler,' said a man with a white cat and a boxer dog.

'I heard he's got a whole squadron of spies intent on infecting our animals,' said an old woman with a Yorkshire terrier.

The queue of people moved steadily forward, while Mr Harris wrestled Tiger, dragged Rose and pulled back Buster. It was turning out to be a less than pleasant experience. But, now that they were here, he was determined to see it through.

The animals in the queue took the experience as an opportunity to sniff at each other and wag their tails, unaware of the terrible fate that awaited them.

Far ahead of him Mr Harris could see people going into the animal centre with their pets, but coming out alone.

'I heard it was two bob to pay,' someone behind him said.

Mr Harris's ears pricked up.

He looked round as a ginger-bearded man with a Dalmatian said: 'As much as that?'

'I thought it was free,' said a woman with a black cat in a cat carrier. The cat hissed at the Dalmatian.

Mr Harris had thought it would be free too and was more than a little disappointed at the thought that it might not be.

'If it wasn't for NARPAC, I'd do it myself,' said a man whose dog looked as though it had recently been in a fight and had a sore on its front leg.

NARPAC were a lot of *busybodies*, in Mr Harris's opinion. They even had voluntary street Animal Guards – *layabouts*, in Mr Harris's opinion – who should have been off fighting rather than sticking their beaky noses into other people's business.

Everyone was supposed to pay a fee to register their pets with NARPAC and you were given a numbered disc: another waste of money that could have been used more productively elsewhere, in Mr Harris's *considered* opinion.

'It's so the owners of lost or injured animals can be traced,' his wife had said when he'd moaned about it.

'Even if they don't want to be,' Mr Harris had retorted.

'The official NARPAC literature says if an animal doesn't have a disc it'll have to be put down.'

Yes, and there'd be no need to pay for it then, thought Mr Harris to himself. The money saved could go towards a beer or two. Looking after animals was thirsty work and he was entitled to a pint.

'I'd do it for a shilling if anyone wants to pay me,' said the man with the injured dog.

Mr Harris had not expected to have to pay out any money when he'd set off that morning. And he didn't want to put his hand in his pocket now. Three of them he'd need to have put down – at three times the cost. It wasn't even as if they were his animals. It wasn't right.

The queue kept moving forward and more people emerged from the animal shelter, petless.

They were getting close to the entrance when Rose started to shake uncontrollably.

'What's got into your dog?' asked the woman with the black cat.

'It's almost as if it knows,' said the man with the injured dog.

'Stop it, you dumb animal,' Mr Harris said. He joggled Rose's lead, but she didn't stop shaking. Rose looked at him with terrified eyes. Now they were closer to the shelter the smell was overpowering. A town pet might not have recognized the smell, but Rose had encountered it countless times on the farm and it filled her with fear. It was the unmistakable smell of death.

The queue advanced, but Rose braced her four legs and refused to move. Mr Harris had to forcibly drag her until he finally got his leg behind her and gave her a sharp nudge. At least the other two were being reasonably well behaved, he consoled himself. But no sooner had he thought this than Buster started whining and then the whine turned into a bark and Rose started barking too – it was almost as if they were warning the other animals not to go inside.

'Be quiet!' Mr Harris shouted at Buster and Rose, and yanked at their leads while struggling to keep a hold on Tiger.

Rose didn't stop barking, but Buster stopped whining, only to throw back his head and howl. Tiger took this opportunity to scratch Mr Harris and with a yowl the cat jumped out of his arms.

'Oh no you don't!' Mr Harris tried to grab Tiger, but as he did so Buster and Rose broke free from their leads.

And now the three pets were running, running as though their lives depended upon it.

Mr Harris stumbled after them, pushing past people and pets. 'Stop, come back!'

The animals didn't hesitate for a second at the sound of his voice.

They raced past the Labrador puppy, who wagged his tail and tried to join them.

'No, Toby!'

Past the miniature poodle, whose owner was now eating a sandwich, past the Siamese cat and the boxer and the whippet and the hundreds of other pets waiting with their owners in the long, long queue.

Buster was in a state of panic as he ran past a Dalmatian that tried to follow him, but was yanked sharply back on his lead. Buster didn't know why they were running; all he knew was that something was very wrong and they had to escape.

'I'll take that little one . . .' said one of the villagers.

'And I'll have that one,' said another.

The youngest of the children were the first to be chosen. Robert frowned. It wasn't right. Little children being given to strangers.

No one wanted Charlie. Finally he was the only one left in the front row and the villagers started picking children from the row behind him.

Charlie wished he'd brought his teddy instead of

the wooden truck he'd chosen to take as the one toy he was allowed to bring.

'I'll have her,' a woman with a scarf over her rollers said, pointing to the girl next to Lucy.

Lucy was more than pleased to see her go.

Miss Hubbard was standing with a middle-aged couple.

'Robert and Lucy Edwards? Are Robert and Lucy Edwards here?' Miss Hubbard asked.

Lucy moved out of the middle line. The pincher girl turned and poked her tongue out at her as she left the chapel.

'We're here,' said Robert, stepping forward.

'This is Mr and Mrs Foster, your grandmother's friends. You'll be going with them,' Miss Hubbard said.

'But where's our grandmother?' Lucy said. 'We thought we were going to be staying with her. Why isn't she here?'

'Is she OK?' Robert asked them.

'Beatrice is . . .' Mrs Foster started to say.

Lucy gave Robert a worried look.

'She'll be fine,' Mr Foster finished. 'Come on, let's get you home.'

Lucy looked back at Charlie, standing all alone and pitiful on the stage.

'Please . . .'

'Yes?' Mrs Foster smiled.

'Could we take him with us? He won't be any

trouble and he can have half my food so he won't cost much. It's just . . .'

'She took a liking to him on the train,' Robert finished for her.

The Fosters looked over at Charlie.

Charlie looked back at them, stuck his thumb in his mouth and sucked it.

Mr and Mrs Foster looked at each other. Lucy waited.

'All right.'

Lucy beckoned to Charlie and he ran off the stage and raced over to them, a smile of delight on his face.

Mr Foster loaded their suitcases in the back of his farm truck and then helped the children up there as well, where there was some sacking for them to sit on.

'We went to pick Beatrice up this morning, to take her to collect you . . .' Mrs Foster said, making herself as comfortable as possible in the front seat. 'She's not been quite herself recently . . .' She gave her husband a knowing look as he climbed into the driver's seat. 'And she didn't feel she was able to come with us.'

'Is Gran ill?' Lucy asked.

'Not exactly . . .' Mr Foster said, looking to his wife questioningly.

She gave him a tiny nod. 'They need to know.'

Mr Foster continued: 'The announcement that we

55

were at war, well, it was too much for her to comprehend . . .'

'You know she lost her only son – your uncle – in the Great War,' Mrs Foster added. 'It was a terrible thing.'

'But that was years ago,' Lucy added. 'Before I was even born.'

'Shh,' Robert told her. 'It takes a long time to recover from something like that.'

'You're right, Robert,' Mrs Foster said kindly. 'So, well . . . we just think it will be too much for her to look after you at the moment.'

'But can we go and see her?' Robert asked.

'Of course – we'll stop by as we're driving back,' Mr Foster said. He started the engine. The truck was noisy and a bit smelly. It wasn't generally used for transporting people.

'Bumpy,' Charlie commented as they left Witherton on the Moor and rattled along country lanes that had grass growing up the middle of them.

Ten minutes later they stopped outside a small thatched cottage. Robert jumped out of the back of the truck and then helped Lucy down. They hurried towards their gran's front door.

'What about me?' Charlie wailed; he didn't want to be left behind.

Mr Foster helped him out.

Robert knocked loudly, then pressed down on the latch and opened the door. No one ever locked their doors in small villages like this. Lucy followed him inside.

'Gran? Gran?' Robert called. There was no reply. Where could she be? He went up the wooden stairs. 'Gran?'

Although her bed had clearly been slept in, their grandmother was nowhere in the house.

'Maybe she went for a walk,' Mr Foster said, arriving at the doorway with Charlie holding his hand tightly. Beatrice had recently been spotted doing an awful lot of walking for a lady of advancing years.

'She could be injured,' Lucy said, worried.

Mr Foster shook his head. 'I'm sure she's fine. She's lived here all her life. It's time we got you home. We'll come back to check on her tomorrow.' He headed back down the stairs with Charlie following obediently.

Robert would really have preferred to see his grandmother now, but he saw the sense in what Mr Foster said. Even when they'd last come to stay at Gran and Grandad's on holiday, his gran had gone off for long walks by herself – sometimes without telling anyone – and then she'd turn up later. It was just one of her little quirks.

Robert nodded. 'Come on,' he said, leading Lucy out of the house and closing the door firmly behind them.

Chapter 7

Tiger's night-time prowls had often extended to the
Wood Green Animal Shelter and beyond, so the
back walls and alleyways were familiar to him as he
led Rose and Buster back to the Edwardses' home.
He was unable to take his usual more direct and
quicker route, due to the dogs being too big and not
agile enough to run along the garden fences or leap
on to shed roofs or even slip unseen through back
gardens.

Buster was wildly excited as soon as he realized
they were almost home, and raced ahead and up the
front garden path, wagging his tail and barking to
let the Edwardses know that he was back and needed
to be let in.

When no one came, he barked again.

Then Tiger miaowed and scratched at the door.
Usually this resulted in someone letting him in. But
not today. He miaowed again, louder. No one came.
Tiger leapt up on to the window ledge, the tip of his
tail twitching as he peered through the window.

Buster barked over and over, his barks becoming desperate. But still no one came.

Rose stood behind them, her head down. She'd had more experience of no one coming, however long she waited.

But Tiger and Buster were not deterred. An alleyway that Tiger knew from his nightly prowls ran along the back of the terraced houses. Tiger led Buster and Rose down it until they came to the Edwardses' back garden. The fence was low and easy for the animals to jump over. Buster ran to the back door, barking to be let into his home. But inside everything was dark and silent.

Michael had promised Robert he would check on his and Lucy's pets while they were away, and Michael was a boy of his word.

The first time he knocked on the Harrises' door there was no reply. Mrs Harris was at work and Mr Harris was at that point struggling to get Buster, Rose and Tiger to the Wood Green Animal Shelter.

The second time Michael knocked, later in the day, Buster and Rose were being led home by Tiger, Mr Harris was drinking his first pint at the Horse and Groom, and Mrs Harris had just arrived home from work. She opened the door to Michael.

'May I help you, dear?' she asked him.

'I'm a friend of Robert Edwards,' Michael

59

explained. 'And I was just wondering how Buster, Rose and Tiger were getting on?'

'Checking up on us?' Mrs Harris asked. She sounded a bit offended.

'No, no,' Michael said quickly; he hadn't meant to appear rude. 'I just wanted to see how they were – I promised Robert I would.'

'Well, I'm afraid they're not here,' Mrs Harris said. 'My husband must have taken them out for a walk.' She had been wondering where they were herself.

'Even Tiger?' Michael said.

'Yes, well, it does seem a little bit unusual,' Mrs Harris said. And, knowing her husband, she silently added to herself that it was in fact extremely unusual for her lazy husband to go for a walk at all. Let alone walk someone else's pets. But the fact was that neither her Harry nor the Edwardses' pets were there, and it seemed to be the only reasonable explanation for their disappearance.

'Would it be all right if I came back later?' Michael asked Mrs Harris.

'Suit yourself,' Mrs Harris said, although she had a growing feeling of unease. She closed the door. What had Harry done now?

'Here we are, home sweet home,' Mr Foster said, as he drew up outside the Devon longhouse, a white-washed thatched cottage that had been built from cob and stone in the fifteenth century.

Robert jumped out of the back of the truck and helped Mr Foster to lift Lucy and Charlie down.

'I'm so hungry my belly's nearly touching my backbone,' Charlie said.

Mrs Foster went in to make some food while Mr Foster showed the children around the farm. He told them how the longhouse once used to provide human and animal accommodation under the same roof.

'You don't mean the cows would live indoors too – with you?' Charlie said.

Mr Foster nodded. That was exactly what he meant. 'And it wasn't so long ago, neither,' he added, and then he grinned at the sight of Charlie's stricken face. 'The cows would be tethered with their heads facing the outside wall and there'd be a central drain down the middle.'

Charlie still didn't look like he quite believed him. 'But you didn't have to sleep with the cows, did you?' he asked. Charlie was so tired that he could have fallen asleep where he stood, but he still didn't think he'd have been able to sleep with a cow snoring next to him.

'Not me,' Mr Foster said. 'I'm not that old, but maybe a hundred years ago, especially in winter, you'd have appreciated the warmth.'

Charlie wasn't sure that he would have. And what if the cow decided to take a bite out of him during the night?

'These cows are known as Ruby Reds,' Mr Foster

told them, rubbing a hand along the side of an auburn-coloured cow with gentle eyes. 'Or Red Ruby Devons, and they're just about the finest breed of cow there is.'

Lucy went to stroke the cow. 'She's beautiful,' she said.

'It's huge,' said Charlie, looking doubtful.

'That's just where you're wrong,' Mr Foster said. 'Ruby Reds are medium-sized cows.'

'Do they bite?' Charlie asked. They definitely looked to him like they might bite.

'No,' Lucy told him. 'They don't bite. They're very gentle, friendly cows.'

Mr Foster had about twenty of them and they fed on the culm pasture grassland.

'The Devon Rubies have lived here for thousands of years and will probably be grazing here long after we've all gone,' he said.

He walked on and the three children followed him. Charlie turned back to look at the cow with the gentle eyes. He was glad they didn't bite, but he wasn't going to put his fingers anywhere near their mouths, just in case.

'Chickens,' Lucy smiled.

Charlie had never seen chickens before and was surprised when Lucy told him that they were where his breakfast eggs came from. He stared at them, wondering how they made eggs.

'You can feed them if you want to,' Mr Foster said.

'Here, throw them a bit of this and watch them peck it up.'

Charlie threw some corn at the chickens and laughed as they ran over, making clucking sounds, and started pecking at it.

'They sure like corn,' he said.

Mr Foster ruffled his hair. 'Which is good because a happy chicken lays good eggs,' he said.

As well as the cows and chickens Mr Foster had lots of sheep that pastured on the adjacent moorland hills, a few pigs that lived in the small orchard and a sheepdog called Molly.

'She looks just like Rose!' Lucy cried with delight, but as soon as she said it she felt a pang of sadness. Was Rose missing her like she was missing Rose? She imagined the loyal collie going from room to room at the Harrises' house looking for her and Robert. Rose always liked it best when they were all together. Now Lucy didn't know when they would all be together again.

'I think you'll find Molly's not nearly as bright as Rose,' Mr Foster said wryly.

Molly was delighted to meet the children and rolled over on to her back. Charlie didn't have a pet at home and was usually a little bit frightened of dogs, but Molly managed to charm him in no time at all.

'What's she doing?' he laughed as Molly lay on her back with her legs in the air having her tummy rubbed by Robert. 'Are you tickling her?'

Molly sneezed and sat up, which made Charlie laugh even more. She went over to him, tail still wagging, and pushed her head under his hand, telling him, as clearly as a dog could, that she'd like a stroke.

Charlie tentatively reached out his hand. 'She feels so soft,' he said in wonder.

'She's not much more than a puppy,' Mr Foster said, and then he added, 'and just about the worst sheepdog I've ever seen, aren't you, Molly?'

Molly wagged her tail at the mention of her name.

'I used to go out with my grandfather and Rose to watch them work the sheep,' Robert said. Rose had always seemed to know exactly what his grandfather wanted her to do – almost before his grandfather had said a word.

Mr Harris returned home at around five o'clock, more than a little drunk, to find a very angry Mrs Harris waiting for him.

'Where are they?' Mrs Harris said.

'Wha–? What you talking about, woman?'

'The Edwardses' pets – where are they?'

'How should I know? Probably ran off.'

Now *he* looked angry, and Mrs Harris thought it best to not say any more. There was a knock at the door.

'Who's that?'

'It'll be that boy again. His dad's part of NARPAC.'

Mr Harris opened the door. 'Yes,' he slurred, looking Michael up and down.

'I'm a friend of Robert Edwards . . .'

'Never heard of him.' Mr Harris started to close the door.

'Wait!' Michael put his foot in the door. Mr Harris looked down at the offending foot and then back up at Michael. 'You were looking after three pets – a collie, a Jack Russell and a ginger tomcat.'

'So what if I was? And I'm not saying I was, mind.'

Michael was sure that if Buster was in the Harrises' house, and able to, he would've come running, barking, to the door.

'Are they here?' Michael removed his foot from the door.

Mr Harris took the opportunity to slam the door shut. 'Mind your own business,' he shouted through the letterbox.

As Michael trudged home, he passed the Edwardses' house, unaware that Buster, Rose and Tiger were there, alone in the back garden.

They'd been there for more than an hour, but still no one had come home or let them in. Rose lay by the back door, her head between her paws. Tiger was beside the ornamental fishpond trying to hook out a goldfish. Buster's playful nature had been severely tested by the trauma of the day, but now it returned. In the late afternoon sun he started digging close to where he'd been excavating on the day the

Anderson Shelter arrived. A few minutes later he pulled out the second of Mr Edwards's slippers, and held it triumphantly between his teeth, muddy and ruined.

Buster looked over at Rose and waggled the slipper tantalizingly, inviting her to chase him for it. Rose saw what he had, but she didn't react. Buster came closer until he was right beside Rose and nudged it at her, urging her to take it. The slipper was too much for Rose to resist, but as soon as she moved and Buster saw that he'd sparked her interest he hopped back from her with it. If she wanted it, she'd have to stand up. In no time at all Rose was chasing Buster around the garden after the slipper. He dropped it and she grabbed it and now Buster was chasing Rose. On they played, turn by turn, until they were both exhausted and lay on the patio, panting.

Tiger, who'd just finished eating the goldfish he'd managed to catch, watched them with an air of disdain, and then got busy methodically washing himself.

All the time the animals played and ate and rested, they listened for the sound of their family returning. But the sound never came.

When Michael got home, he was greeted by a boisterous array of happy pets. As neighbours and friends had had to leave London, many of them had asked if Michael's family would take care of their pets, and now Michael's house was full to over-flowing.

As well as cats and dogs there were also a number of caged birds, including two cockatoos, a parrot and three budgies.

When his father came home, Michael told him what had happened at the Harrises'. 'I'm sure he's done something to those animals. He acted really shifty when I spoke to him,' he said.

Mr Ward accepted a much-needed cup of tea from his wife and said, 'He'll almost certainly have taken them to the Wood Green Animal Shelter.' His expression told Michael that he too feared the worst.

Michael was furious at the thought of the pets having been put down, and that he'd been unable to stop it from happening.

'Isn't there a record of all the animals that have been killed? Couldn't we check somehow?' he asked his father.

Mr Ward shrugged his shoulders. 'I can look into it. There are supposed to be accurate records kept, but this is wartime,' he said. 'Sometimes things go by the by. Also, I doubt very much that this Mr Harris would register using his real name, don't you?'

'Well, can't you write their names down in your registration book?' Michael urged him. 'There's a chance that they might be still alive.'

His father shook his head. 'They didn't go missing in an air raid, son.'

But Michael didn't think that should matter. The main thing was that they were missing and the more people who knew about it, the better.

'There's going to be thousands of strays in London soon. If they didn't have identification tags, then how is anyone supposed to guess that they're your friends' pets? It's impossible,' Mr Ward said.

'There must be *something* we can do.'

'We'll keep our eyes and ears open and maybe we'll get lucky. But that's all we can do,' Mr Ward said grimly. He sighed. Being an animal lover could be tough, especially when people were so unthinkingly cruel to them.

Michael fed some carrot to the cockatoo.

'There are so many strays already wandering the streets,' his father said. 'It might not have been the worst thing if he did have them put down. Better than them dying of starvation or getting knocked over by a passing vehicle and curling up somewhere to die in agony.'

But Michael wasn't really listening to the last part of what his father said. He was thinking that if Mr Harris had let the pets go, then they might have returned to the Edwardses' home.

'I'm going round to the Edwardses',' he said, and headed for the door.

His mother stopped him. 'Not now you're not,' she told him. 'Now you'll have your dinner and then you'll help clean out the birds' cages.'

'But –'

'And there'll be no buts about it. Tomorrow will be soon enough to go back there.'

After they'd washed their hands, Robert, Lucy and Charlie sat down at a table that was filled with food.

'Are we having a feast?' Charlie said. He'd never seen this much food on a table before.

Mrs Foster smiled. 'I wasn't quite sure what you might like to eat so I thought I'd put out lots of different things.'

There were ham and cheese sandwiches, pasties, a cake, some scones with jam and a jug of cream.

Mrs Foster looked on as Charlie tucked in. He certainly did have a large and healthy appetite for a five-year-old.

After supper Robert went back to his gran's house with Mr Foster. It was almost dark. They could see a flickering candle in the window so they knew Beatrice must have returned. But she'd wedged something behind the door so they couldn't get in.

'Go away!' she called out when Mr Foster rapped on the door. 'Go away or I'll shoot you.'

'Gran – it's me, Robert.'

But Gran didn't seem to hear him. 'Go away!' she screamed.

Robert looked at Mr Foster. 'What should we do?' he asked him.

Mr Foster thought for a moment. 'I think it would be better if we came back in the morning,' he said.

When no one had returned by nightfall, Rose, Buster and Tiger went into the dark and damp Anderson Shelter to sleep.

It was the first time Tiger and Buster had had to spend the night outside. Tiger's night-time adventures were not usually that long and there was always a warm bed to return home to if the weather turned bad.

Now there was no one, and no dinner either. Buster whimpered with hunger; he'd never gone without a meal before and apart from the scraps Mrs Harris had given him he'd had nothing to eat. He cuddled up to Rose for warmth. Tiger scratched at the ground a little way away from them to make himself a rough earth-bed to sleep in. Once this was completed to his satisfaction he lay down in it. But the lonely earth-bed was cold and Tiger missed the warmth of Lucy. Sometime during the night he left his spot and curled up with the two dogs and the three of them slept huddled together.

At the Fosters' house Lucy lay in the cold, unfamiliar room and wanted more than anything to be in her own room in her own bed with Tiger snuggled up beside her, his furry head nestled into her neck and a purr rumbling deep in his throat.

A tear rolled down Lucy's face as she stared at the flock wallpaper and thumped the lumpy pillow to try to make it a little more comfortable. The bed was harder than she was used to and the room smelt dusty and musty, as if it was hardly ever used.

She missed her mum and she missed her dad, but most of all she missed Tiger, Buster and Rose. She missed them all so badly it was like an ache within her, and she didn't think she'd ever be able to drop off to sleep.

In the room next door Charlie had no such problems. He'd crawled into bed in the room he was to share with Robert and had fallen instantly asleep on his tummy, exhausted from the long day and all that had happened.

Robert lay in his bed with his hands behind his head, staring up at the ceiling. He wondered where Dad was and imagined him flying the Blenheim over enemy territory, taking the photos that would help Britain to win the war.

Charlie started snoring and for such a small boy he made quite a racket. Robert didn't expect to get much sleep, but the monotony of the snores was oddly soothing and soon he was out cold.

Chapter 8

Rose was stirring well before sunrise and it was five o'clock when the three pets left the Anderson Shelter.

Only Rose had ever lived in Devon. Buster and Tiger had both been born and lived their whole lives in North London. Now, though, they didn't seem to have a home. The people that had made the house theirs were gone and they didn't know where they'd gone to. They were unsettled and hungry.

Rose might have chosen to slip quietly out of the Anderson Shelter and start her long journey alone, but the others awoke as soon as she moved and were right behind her as she left the garden and set off down the road.

Rose, for all her purposeful tread, did not know the way from London to Devon. She just knew that that was where she was going. She would have to trust her gut and her instinct to show her the path. The other two needed someone to lead them, and so they followed Rose because she seemed to have somewhere to go.

Rose took them across Alexandra Park, where Buster found the smell of the horses that had raced there intriguing. He would have spent far longer sniffing the grass where the horses had been, but the other two moved onwards and he didn't want to be left behind.

The oak and beech trees shaded them at Queen's Wood and now it was the squirrels that distracted Buster and he almost lost the other two when he ran down an overgrown path after one. The squirrel ran up a tree and Buster barked at it, and then ran back the way he'd come – only now there were two paths. He sat down and howled and had almost given up when the undergrowth parted and Rose and Tiger were there.

They stopped for a rest and a long cool drink at the outdoor swimming ponds on Hampstead Heath.

Thirst quenched, Buster and Rose played while Tiger stretched and watched them chew at each other's ears and forelegs before chasing one another over the grass.

The trio of pets trotted through the London streets, far less obvious at this early hour than they might have been later in the day. From Parliament Hill, Rose led them over Primrose Hill and in through the gates of Regent's Park.

Buster had always been very interested in the ducks that quacked noisily on the lake at the local park that Robert and Lucy took him to sometimes.

But that was as far as his knowledge of bodies of water went.

He'd never been allowed to plunge into the enticing water because Robert always put him on his lead when they got close to it.

Rose now stared intently at the water in the boating lake at Regent's Park and Buster watched her, his head turning from the water to Rose and back again.

Rose barely moved at all, her eyes fixed on the shadows that weaved in and out just below the surface of the lake.

And then suddenly, to Buster's utter astonishment, with a giant leap she was off the bank and had splashed into the water. A few seconds later she doggy-paddled to the side with a flapping fish in her mouth which she proceeded to eat, as Buster and Tiger looked on.

Buster might not have been in a lake or been fishing before, but he was a quick learner. He watched the moving shadows under the water and ran along the path round the lake, past the empty boats, barking at them – not quite brave enough to leap in the water yet, but wanting a fish to eat, definitely wanting a fish.

Tiger watched the water from the rowboat launching pad. He kept very still, as he always did when he was hunting and about to pounce. Running about and yapping as Buster was doing would do nothing but scare the prey away.

While Rose finished the tail of her fish-feast and Buster stopped running and barking and lay down on the ground and whined in disappointed misery, Tiger waited. Although, like all housecats, he had the ability to swim, he didn't like to get wet. He'd decided his dinner could come to him. He didn't have to wait long for a smaller fish to swim past his waiting-place. Tiger batted at the fish with his paw. The dazed fish tried to swim on, but it was too late. Tiger pulled it on to the side and started eating while the fish was still flapping.

Buster, seeing Rose and now Tiger eating fish, raced into the lake and swam for the first time in his life, doggy-paddling in circles. When it came to fish, he didn't yet have the hunting skills that the other two had. But his hunger was just as well satisfied by the rat that peered inquisitively at the small, splashing dog, only to find itself clamped in the jaws of a jubilant Buster.

No sooner had Buster finished eating the rat than two swans came gliding towards him. None of the three animals had seen swans before. Rose and Tiger were instinctively wary. Tiger tried to look bigger and more intimidating by arching his back, and Rose's hackles went up. But Buster had no fear of the territorial swans and barked excitedly, jumping into the water to greet them.

The swans hissed and headed purposefully towards the small dog.

Rose barked a warning to Buster and when Buster didn't respond quickly enough she barked again, more urgently. Buster clambered out of the water just in time and shook himself at the water's edge before running off after the other two.

The pets emerged from Regent's Park alongside the gates of London Zoo, ignorant of the fact that the animals that lived there were today being transported to the rural safety of Whipsnade Zoo. Buster ran straight into the path of an elephant being led along by its keeper. He'd never encountered such a large animal, and cowered away from it in shock.

A junior zookeeper with a shock of red hair came running over to the man with the elephant.

'What about the snakes in the reptile house? They're still there – no one's moved them. And the spiders and scorpions have been forgotten.'

'They're not coming with us,' the older man told him.

'But . . .'

'They'll be chloroformed. They'd be too great a threat if the Germans got their hands on them.'

'But they can't just . . . that's not right!'

'This is war, boy.'

The elephant gave a final hurrah as it left.

The animals moved on, navigating their way by pure good luck across the busier roads and down past Buckingham Palace. The pets didn't notice the Union Jack flapping high up on the flag-pole, but it signalled to all who saw it that the king and queen were at home and refusing to be evacuated.

Even as people started to move about the busy city, the streets were much less populated than they would normally have been at the weekend. No one had the time to be a tourist any more. And no one had the time to pay attention to three stray animals.

Down in Devon Robert and Charlie were woken by the sound of a cockerel crowing.

'What's that?' Charlie said, his eyes wide with fear. He'd never heard anything like it before.

'It's just a cockerel,' Robert replied sleepily.

'What's a cock-le?' Charlie asked.

'Cock-er-el – it's a male chicken.'

Charlie frowned. 'Chickens make clucking sounds.'

Robert threw off his covers. 'Come on, I'll show you,' he said, and the two boys went out into the farmyard in their pyjamas.

Charlie was very impressed with the cockerel. 'He's so noisy!' he said. Then he thought for a bit. 'Sometimes my mum says I'm too noisy. You don't . . .' He looked at Robert for reassurance. He was suddenly on the edge of tears. 'You don't think she sent me away because I was too noisy?'

'No,' Robert told him. 'It was because Hitler might be invading and there could be bombs and she didn't want you to get hurt.'

*

Back inside the thatched cottage, Lucy missed the usual comforting morning purr of Tiger when she woke up.

He'd always been there in her bed beside her for as long as she could remember. She threw back the covers, padded over to her suitcase and pulled out the drawing pad and pencils she'd brought with her as the single 'toy' evacuees were allowed. She began to draw and didn't stop until Mrs Foster called out, 'Breakfast's ready!'

She raced down the stairs as Robert and Charlie came back inside. Mrs Foster had made a huge breakfast of bacon, eggs, mushrooms, tomatoes, sausages and fried bread.

'I hope you're hungry,' she said.

'I'm always hungry,' Charlie told her, as he tucked in.

After breakfast Michael headed down the streets to Robert's house. The net curtains of number 9, the Harrises' house, twitched as he passed.

The more he thought about it, the more it seemed a real possibility that the animals might have gone back to the Edwardses' house. But when he got there he found the house securely locked up. He peered in through the windows, but could see nothing. He went down the alleyway and climbed over the fence into the back garden.

No pets came to greet him as he'd hoped they would. He tried calling them anyway: 'Buster, Rose . . . Tiger?'

The pets didn't come running. Michael sighed. Then he remembered the Anderson Shelter and headed over to it, walking past the slipper that Buster and Rose had played with the evening before, without realizing what it was.

None of the animals were inside the Anderson Shelter, although he could see the soil had been freshly scratched to make a sleeping patch. He crouched down to take a closer look. The patch didn't mean that Tiger had slept there. It was just as likely to have been a stray. But as he looked more closely he saw that there was something on the ground, partly embedded in the soil. He picked it up and it made a sound. There was no mistaking it. It was the bell from Tiger's collar.

Maybe Tiger had slept here before the Edwardses left for Devon, or maybe he had come back to the house since. Michael knew that cats often returned to their old homes and it wasn't far from number 9 to number 15.

He took it outside to have a better look. The bell still looked shiny. If Tiger had lost it some time ago, it would have turned dull. Michael waited, but Tiger didn't return, and finally he gave up and headed home, taking the bell with him.

Number 9's curtains twitched again as he passed.

Inside, Mrs Harris whispered to her husband. 'He's coming back.'

'He's not coming here, is he?' said Mr Harris.

Mrs Harris gave him a look. He still hadn't told her what he'd done with the animals and he seemed to have no intention of doing so.

'No, gone past,' she said.

'Interfering NARPAC busybodies. The government has given people like him far too much power. Intimidating innocent folks like us,' Mr Harris complained, and went back to his boiled egg and tea.

Mrs Harris resisted saying that she didn't think her husband had ever been the innocent victim he sometimes liked to portray himself as. In fact, she couldn't even imagine him being innocent when he was a baby. He'd probably had a rattle-robbing trade going on. But she didn't say anything. It was generally wise not to say too much when Harry was around.

At Trafalgar Square the animals stopped, not far from the four magnificent bronze lions that guarded the foot of Nelson's column. But it wasn't the statues that made first Tiger and then Buster and finally Rose stop. It was the pigeons, which to Tiger meant one thing – food. He tried to sneak up on them before pouncing on his chosen victim. But Buster had never seen so many birds in one place before.

He was overcome with excitement and raced at the pigeons, barking wildly. The pigeons did what pigeons do and flew off – but not too far – before settling down again. The Trafalgar Square pigeons were used to being chased and scattered by the tourists that came to see them. They'd had countless children charging through their number and they weren't fazed by one small dog.

Rose's herding instinct came to the fore and before she knew it she was racing after the birds too.

Tiger, all too aware that making a commotion was not the way to get a meal, crouched low and waited. In just a few seconds his patience was rewarded. A pigeon, avoiding the yapping Buster and the herding Rose, fluttered down without realizing Tiger was there until it was too late.

Buster and Rose stopped running after the birds and watched Tiger eating. They were hungry too. The pigeon was large and Tiger could not eat it all. He nudged what was left over to Buster and Rose and then scrupulously washed his face and paws as he watched the dogs tear at the carcass. But it wasn't enough; however, the pigeons soon came back. Buster and Rose chased after them again and a second pigeon was caught and devoured.

Finally full, the animals' attention now turned to quenching their thirst and they had a long cool drink from the fountain. The day had turned warm and Rose cooled her tired paws in the water.

Then the animals slept for a while in the shade of the stone lions and woke to the sight of an elephantine grey barrage balloon floating above them. Buster had never seen a moving thing so large and ran and hid under a bench. Rose, used to animals larger than herself and less readily intimidated, watched warily till it was out of sight. Tiger licked his paws.

It was twilight by the time they crossed the cobblestones of Covent Garden and ventured into the backstreets beyond. Soon there was a new and enticing smell just ahead of them. The smell of meat from the market at Smithfield. The market wasn't open on Sundays, but there was still meat waste to scavenge, and Tiger added a mouse or two to his own supper.

They might have chosen to spend the night there, but a security guard spotted them and threw a bucket of water over them.

'Get lost before I skin the lot of you!'

Drenched, but with their stomachs full, the animals pressed on.

When Mr Foster took Robert and Lucy to see their grandmother, the old lady seemed to have no recollection of refusing to open the door to Robert the evening before or indeed of shouting at him to go away.

'Robert and dear Lucy,' she cried with delight

when she saw them. 'What on earth are you doing here? Are you on holiday? Where's your mother?'

Mr Foster smiled ruefully at Robert. On the way back last night he'd told Robert that it might be better if he and his sister and Charlie stayed with them for the time being – even if Beatrice said they could stay with her.

'Your grandmother . . . well, she hasn't been finding it easy to cope recently. One day she seems fine and the next day she's not so good.'

Robert quickly worked out that Mr Foster had clearly been underplaying whatever it was that was wrong with his gran. 'We're staying with Mr and Mrs Foster,' he said.

'Really?'

Lucy gave Robert a look. He knew she wanted to stay with their grandmother and in lots of ways so did he; they hardly knew the Fosters, after all. But it seemed wiser to stay where they were, at least for the moment.

'Yes – but we'll be coming over to see you every day,' Robert said.

'See you tomorrow then,' Gran said, and got busy with the hole she was digging.

'What's that for?' Lucy asked her.

'Never you mind,' Beatrice said, and carried on digging.

Robert shook his head at Lucy and gestured that it was time to leave. 'See you tomorrow, Gran,' he said.

Beatrice kept on digging.

'What's wrong with her?' Lucy asked her brother on the way back to the Fosters'.

Mr Foster overheard her. 'It's the war,' he said. 'For people who lived through and lost people they loved in the last war it's too much to accept that now we're in another one.' He knew Beatrice wasn't the only one to be affected in this way, not by a long shot, and who could blame her really? A person could only take so much.

It was nightfall and the animals' energy was now all but exhausted from the long day. Dogged determination and the need to find somewhere safe and dry to sleep kept them moving forward.

They'd only just dried off from their market drenching when a violent storm soaked them all over again. The day that had started with so much promise was now turning into a night of despair. Heads down, they padded on through the relentless rain and strong wind. They crossed London Bridge, barely aware of the dark water of the River Thames flowing below them or of the floating hospital ship that glided past.

The young man on the bridge stared down into the water and paid no attention to the three sodden pets that passed him. Private Matthews couldn't face being in the war. He knew that at some point he'd be expected to shoot a Jerry or be shot by one – and he couldn't. Nor did he see how anyone else could do it. How could one person take the life of another person who'd done him no harm?

But he was the only one he knew who felt that way and he was jeered at when he tried to speak up – so he'd shut up. One of his workmates had even muttered the word 'coward' – and perhaps he was. All he knew for sure was that he couldn't go to war. He just couldn't.

The cold water seemed so inviting, comforting even, that he found himself drawn towards it and the light . . . falling, falling.

The icy coldness of the Thames hit his body with a punch of reality. His arms flailed in the water and he swallowed mouthfuls of the filthy stuff.

Just seconds later Mrs Edwards, working on the floating hospital ship she'd been assigned to, threw the life-ring to the figure in the water. Two of her volunteer nurses raced on deck behind her, hardly able to believe that they had really seen what they thought they'd seen.

'Grab hold of that!' a voice yelled, as the life-ring was thrown. And suddenly Private Matthews knew that he didn't want to die, he didn't want to die at all, not now, not like this.

Private Matthews grabbed hold of the life-ring like a drowning man, which is really what he was, and the ring was pulled hand over fist to the hospital ship. He was pulled on board and wrapped in a blanket.

'Lucky we came along when we did,' said a motherly-looking nurse with a kind face. 'Otherwise who knows what injury you might have suffered from your . . . *fall*.'

Private Matthews shivered inside the blanket. Attempted suicide was a crime. He could go to jail or at the very least be fined for it. A volunteer handed him a cup of hot chocolate, which he sipped gratefully, the hot liquid warming him from the inside out.

'Bridges can get very slippery in the rain,' added the nurse, with a kind but knowing look.

Indeed.

The matron came forward with a thermometer. 'Open wide,' she said.

'Where am I?' Private Matthews mumbled with the instrument stuck in his mouth.

'Floating hospital,' said Mrs Edwards. 'Not many of these about yet.'

'It's like a ship of angels,' Private Matthews said, and the volunteer nurses grinned.

'We aim to please,' one of them laughed.

'Well, you should be thanking *someone* that Nurse Edwards here saw you fall,' said the matron, removing the thermometer and checking the reading. 'Not many people take a swim in the Thames and survive.'

Private Matthews looked around at the nurses. Without them . . . well, he didn't like to think what would've happened.

He was their first patient, they told him as he climbed into the hospital bed.

'Although we expect to end up with lots more if Mr Hitler has his way.'

Private Matthews closed his eyes and drifted off to sleep to the sound of the boat's motor. It was the first time in over a week that he'd really slept, and there were no nightmares that night.

Chapter 9

After crossing London Bridge, Buster, Rose and Tiger entered South London and wound their way down dark, deserted streets, looking but not finding anywhere to stop and sleep. Occasionally they met another cat on a night-time prowl. One ginger tom snarled at Tiger, daring him to fight, but when Tiger responded in kind he turned tail and ran away.

A warehouse yard seemed the perfect sleeping place, but a guard-dog barked at them and bared its teeth, so they moved on. They stopped to shelter in a graveyard, only to have a homeless man throw an empty bottle at them, so they moved on again.

Eventually, they stumbled upon some railway tracks and followed them as if they were a trail of breadcrumbs, too tired to decide on their own direction. But they were soaked through from the storm, shivering and exhausted. Their paws were cut and sore and they needed to find somewhere dry to sleep, and fast.

At Ladywell they found an empty train carriage

and crept inside it. Tiger had enough energy left to jump into the net overhead luggage rack. Buster and Rose lay on the floor near to the window, neither choosing to lie on the more comfortable bench seats that were available.

When a whistle and a shunt woke them the next morning it was with a shock. Rose was immediately awake, but stayed very still. Tiger struggled to get his paw out of the rope holes of the luggage rack and decided to give up and stay where he was. Buster ran to the door, wagging his tail.

The carriage door had been open when they'd crept in last night. Now it was closed. When the door opened, Buster backed away, but couldn't quite manage to hide in time. Rose tensed and a growl rumbled in her throat.

'Hello, old chap,' said a friendly voice, seeing Buster sitting before him. A young airman wearing a brand-new uniform came in and closed the door behind him. His eyes widened when he saw Rose there as well, and widened even more as he went to put his hand luggage on the rack and spotted Tiger.

Tiger miaowed and Officer Cadet Joe Lawson realized the luggage rack, which had made a comfortable bed to start with, was now behaving like a cat trap instead. He freed Tiger's paw and the cat immediately jumped out and down on to the comfortable bench seat to greet his rescuer.

Joe laughed. 'Oh, you are a beauty and don't you

know it,' he said, as he stroked the cat. Tiger purred. It had been too long since he'd been stroked. 'Let me see that,' Joe said, noting Tiger's cut paw. Lucky he had his first-aid kit in his bag.

He was just reaching for it when there was a knock on the outside of the carriage door. Buster raced towards it, but Joe managed to step in front of him and got to it before it could be fully opened.

'Morning, Officer,' said the ruddy-faced conductor, observing the young man's uniform.

'Morning,' Joe replied, his heart beating very fast. He looked the conductor in the eye, willing him not to look down because if he did so, he'd see Buster trying to poke his head through his legs.

'Just checking everything is all right?'

'Yes, quite all right, thank you. I –'

'Conductor!' a commanding voice down the corridor called. 'Conductor!'

'Right you are, Officer,' the conductor said, and hurried off to see who was calling him.

Joe breathed out, closed the door and looked round at Tiger and Rose. Buster wagged his tail at him, head cocked to one side, one ear up and one ear down.

'That was close,' he said.

Rose thumped her tail and Buster stood on his back legs, putting his forepaws on the man's legs. The dogs' tails wagged in unison.

'Now, who'd like to share my sandwiches? My mother always makes enough for a whole battalion,'

Joe said, opening his canvas kitbag. "'You never know when you'll get a chance to eat next," she says.'

The animals were more than willing to help him, and the train journey from London to Kent – Rose's second trip on a steam train, but Buster and Tiger's first – passed most pleasantly.

Down in Devon Robert and Lucy soon adjusted to life on Mr and Mrs Foster's farm, although they missed their parents and pets terribly. In desperation Lucy wrote to Mrs Harris to find out how the animals were getting on:

Dear Mrs Harris,
I hope you are well and that Tiger, Rose and Buster are being good. Robert and I are fine in Devon. Tiger loves to play with feathers. Please would you give him this one to play with?
I would love to hear any news of them and how they are all getting on.

Yours sincerely,
Lucy Edwards

She popped the long pheasant feather she'd found into the envelope and sealed it.

Her bedroom walls were now half covered with sketches of Tiger, Rose and Buster. Tiger featured in more drawings than the other two as Lucy found cats easier to draw, so the pictures she did of him usually turned out better. There would have been more, but she'd run out of drawing paper.

'Oh my, look at all these,' Mrs Foster said, coming into Lucy's room with her clean clothes.

'That's Tiger,' Lucy said, pointing to his picture. 'And this one's Buster.'

'He looks like a mischievous one,' Mrs Foster said.

Lucy grinned. 'He is!' she agreed. 'And this one's –'

'Rose,' Mrs Foster said. 'I've known Rose since she was a puppy. She came from a litter up at Moorvale Farm and she must have been only two weeks old when I first saw her. She didn't even have her eyes open.'

'Tell me more about what Rose was like as a puppy,' Lucy said.

'Well, she was a pretty little thing, very intelligent and very inquisitive. One day, when she must have been only seven weeks old, they thought they'd lost her – looked everywhere they did, only to find her curled up with the lamb they were hand-rearing.'

Lucy grinned.

'Oh,' Mrs Foster smiled as she remembered, 'and she gave you her paw in the sweetest way, almost as if it was in slow motion and a very serious affair. People were always asking her to "shake hands". Most dogs do it quick, but not Rose.'

Lucy couldn't wait to see Rose again and try asking her to shake hands.

'We'd have taken her, you know. By eight weeks old I could see there was something special about her, and to be honest I'd fallen for her. I was looking forward to bringing her home with us, but on the morning we went up to Moorvale Farm to say that we'd like to have her, we found that she'd already been taken. She became your grandfather's dog, but I always had a special place for her in my heart.'

'Sevenoaks Station, alight here for Sevenoaks Station,' the announcer said, as the train slowed down and stopped.

'This is me,' Joe said, picking up his bags. He wished he could take the animals with him, but there was no room for three pets on the airbase.

He closed the door securely behind him as he left the compartment. Buster whimpered, and went to the door and pawed at it.

'Have a pleasant day, Officer,' the conductor said, as Joe left the train.

Buster sat back on his haunches and stared at the door, his head cocked to one side, waiting for Officer Cadet Lawson to come back.

The whistle blew and the train was just about to leave the station when the animals' compartment door opened again.

Buster jumped up and wagged his tail, but it wasn't

the kind airman returning. Their next prospective travelling companion was no animal lover and she gave a shriek that brought the conductor running to her aid.

'What on earth . . .' he said.

The animals raced past him as he made a grab for them and missed, and then there was chaos as they ran down the corridor, dodging past surprised passengers who got in their way, with the conductor determinedly behind them.

He managed to corner them at the end of the train.

'Now I've got you!' he gasped.

The conductor tried to grab Buster's collar just as a latecomer opened the carriage door, and Buster managed to dodge past him and jump out of the train. Then the conductor tried to catch Tiger by the tail, but cats can be as slippery as eels when they need to be, and Tiger was no exception.

Rose slunk past the conductor unseen and out of the train, while the man was getting more and more tangled up with Tiger.

'Yeowch! The beast scratched me,' the conductor yelled, as Tiger leapt out of the train after his companions.

Hearing his friend's yell, the coal stoker grabbed a large piece of coal and threw it at the ginger cat. It was hard to say who was more surprised when he scored a direct hit.

'Gotcha!' the stoker said, as the coal landed squarely on Tiger's back, knocking him over.

Tiger gave a squeal of pain. But he leapt up immediately and ran out of the station after the other two. The three animals ran and ran until they were far away from the station, adrenalin and fear driving them on.

As the sun set, they came to a wooded area and stopped at a stream for a drink. Tiger climbed up a tree to sleep, while the other two settled down at its base.

At first the woodland night sounds disturbed all of them. Even Rose had not been out in the countryside all night before. The screech of an owl, the cry of a fox and a badger that rustled past all filled them with fear. But when no other animal came close enough to be seen, they finally fell fast asleep.

The dawn brought a beautiful pink sunrise and the wood was shrouded in mist. In his tree Tiger stretched, then noticed a nest just above him. It was breakfast time. He slunk up another branch to investigate, ignoring the pain from where the coal had hit him the day before.

Tiger had almost reached the nest when the mother bird saw him. She squawked and flew at him. Tiger swiped at her with his paw. The bird flew to a higher branch out of his reach, but she didn't want to lose her eggs and so she squawked and flew at Tiger again. Tiger batted her away and lowered his head towards the egg prize that would soon be his. In desperation the bird dive-bombed him.

The crow's squawking brought its mate flying back, and now both birds dive-bombed Tiger. The ferocity of the attack caught Tiger by surprise, and as cat and crows fought, the nest became dislodged and fell to the ground where the two dogs gobbled down the eggs.

Tiger saw a rabbit on the ground and raced down the tree and across the woodland after it, only to have the rabbit disappear into its burrow.

Hungry and sore, he slunk back to Buster and Rose. Finding food was becoming an exhausting challenge – and it was one that none of the animals had had to face before.

So many children had been evacuated to the area that the small village school couldn't cope with the number. Not only were there not enough desks, there were also not enough books and not even enough paper or pencils to go round. The school resorted to using chalk and easels, but supplies were woefully inadequate even of these. It was decided that half the children should go to school in the morning and the other half in the afternoon.

Lucy was placed with the rest of the evacuee children. She wasn't pleased when she saw that the 'pincher' girl was in her class. She'd hoped that the chapel was the last time she'd have to see her. No such luck.

All the other children in Lucy's new class knew each other already because they'd all come from the same South London school. They'd already made their own friends.

Lucy felt isolated as the rest of her classmates stared at her. She tried to pretend she didn't care that she didn't have any friends. But she did care really. She cared a lot.

Her class was assigned Miss Hubbard as their teacher.

'Now, Lucy, isn't it?' Miss Hubbard said, on the first day.

Lucy nodded.

'Why don't you go and sit over there.' Miss Hubbard pointed to an empty chair next to a boy who had his finger up his nose.

Lucy could feel everyone staring at her as she walked to her place. She didn't like it and wished she could be back at her old school.

'Pick up your knitting needles. We're going to be making RAF crew scarves, gloves and balaclavas for the war effort,' Miss Hubbard said.

Lucy wrapped the grey wool she'd been given round her needle, thinking how much Tiger would have loved to play with the wool, and a tear dropped on to her knitting.

'What's the matter with you?' the girl behind her said, giving her a poke.

'Nothing.' Lucy did her best to ignore her. But it wasn't easy.

At breaktime the girl deliberately shoved past her, almost knocking her over, and when the bell rang and they all lined up, the girl was standing behind her and pulled her hair.

Lucy clenched her fist tight. She knew that she had to stay out of trouble, and she was doing her best, but it was very hard not to retaliate. Instead she turned round and glared at the girl, who merely pulled a face back at her. As they filed into the classroom Lucy made a silent wish. *Please let us go home soon.*

Chapter 10

The smell coming from the slightly open window of the large country house was so tantalizingly mouth-watering that no cat, let alone a hungry cat like Tiger, could have resisted it.

Tiger jumped on to the windowsill and peered in through the kitchen window, his tail twitching. Rose and Buster sat below the window and sniffed the air. The windowsill was too high above the ground for them to jump up to it, but the smell was almost as enticing to them as it was to Tiger. Rose's stomach rumbled with hunger and a string of drool stretched from Buster's mouth to the ground.

The smell that was so delicious was the aroma of freshly caught salmon cooking. Tiger, still on the windowsill, gave a miaow of pure longing and was shocked when a bald man with piercing light blue eyes suddenly appeared at the glass and stared out at him.

'Hello there, my beauty,' the man said, and he pushed the white lattice-framed window up further.

Tiger had not forgotten his last human encounter,

which had ended with a lump of coal hitting his back. But somehow he knew this man was different. This man was a cat lover.

The man's pudgy fingers reached out and stroked Tiger, and Tiger could feel all the worry of the last few days dissolving. He rubbed his chin against the man's hand and purred with pleasure.

'Oh, Winston, not another cat!' a voice said.

Tiger froze but Winston's hand didn't stop stroking him, not even for one second. 'Yes, and isn't he a beauty,' Winston said. 'Bring over some of that salmon. I suspect he's hungry.'

A moment later a small plate of still-warm salmon was put on the windowsill next to Tiger.

'Go on, then,' Winston told him.

Tiger didn't need to be asked twice. The salmon was gone in no time at all and Tiger put his head to one side, looked at Winston, and miaowed hopefully for more.

Winston laughed. 'More salmon and make it quick,' he said.

Tiger was in heaven. Salmon and someone's fingers that stroked him in just the right way.

'Shut the window. I don't like flies in my kitchen,' the other voice said.

Winston lifted Tiger into the kitchen and pulled down the window behind him.

Outside Buster gave a whimper of disappointment, but no one heard him.

In the kitchen Tiger finished off his second plate of salmon. His stomach was now very full.

'Come on, Cat,' Winston said, and Tiger obediently followed the plump bald man out of the kitchen and down the passageway.

Other people stopped to admire Tiger as he walked behind the man.

'That's a fine-looking cat you have there, Mr Churchill.'

'A very fine cat indeed,' Winston agreed. 'He came to the kitchen window and asked to be let in.'

Winston opened the door to a room that smelt of leather and cigar smoke, and Tiger sauntered in.

'Now, let's see what's been happening in the world.'

Winston sat down at his desk and lit a large cigar before starting to read the official papers in front of him.

Tiger hopped up on to the desk to join him and Winston didn't seem to mind at all.

'Now what shall I call you?' Winston said to his new cat. 'You really are a most magnificent specimen. Although you could do with a bit of feeding up. Hmm, I know, how about Jock?'

Tiger purred as Winston rubbed him behind his ears, which Winston took as being Tiger's approval of his new name.

'Yes, Jock it is then,' he said.

Tiger bumped his head against Winston's hand, hoping for more ear-rubbing. Winston duly obliged.

Later, when Winston moved to one of the leather armchairs, he patted his knees so that Tiger knew he was being invited to join him, and he hopped up into Winston's lap, turned round a few times to ensure he was in the most comfortable spot, and fell fast asleep.

'That's it, Jock,' Winston said, to the sleeping Tiger, as he read through his correspondence. 'You have a nice rest.'

Safe and warm and with his belly full, Tiger slept on and on.

Outside the kitchen window Rose and Buster waited for Tiger to come back, but when he didn't and the window remained firmly closed, the two dogs went off to explore the large garden by themselves. As soon as Buster spotted the pond he was drawn to it and Rose followed him. The pond was shallow, with lily-pads growing on it and large stepping-stones across it. But, more importantly, the pond was full of large black-spotted golden and white and peach-coloured fish. If they couldn't have freshly cooked salmon, then they would catch their own fish.

After checking that there was no one approaching, the two dogs crossed the stones to the middle of the pond and slipped into the water. Working as a team, Buster and Rose corralled the koi carp into a corner of the pond and then dragged one to the side.

They froze as a lady came out to scatter bread,

cake crumbs and bacon rind for the birds – if she'd looked their way, she'd have seen them with fish remnants in front of them. But fortunately she didn't look, and when she'd gone Buster and Rose ate the bird food too.

Then Buster found a strand of discarded rope and he and Rose had a wild, growling game of tug in the rose garden.

As the sun set, it grew colder and lights appeared in the house. The two dogs stared at them as if transfixed. But they didn't approach.

A broken wooden door led them inside a disused, dilapidated potting shed that kept them warm and dry for the night.

Winston liked to keep regular hours, and Tiger found that Winston's routine suited him perfectly. After a few days spent at Chartwell, Tiger was so attuned to this routine that it was as though he'd never lived anywhere else. Winston woke at 7.30 and had his breakfast brought to him in bed, as usual. Tiger also remained on the bed, where he'd spent the night, as usual, and ate his breakfast of salmon from a bowl on a silver tray.

Breakfast finished, Tiger curled up and went back to sleep for a few more hours while Winston read his mail and all the national newspapers and dictated to his secretaries, who scribbled down his words in their notebooks and gave Tiger strokes.

At 11.00 Tiger went out in the garden for a prowl, but not for long. Winston came looking for him after half an hour.

'Jock, Jock, where are you?'

Tiger ran to him and they wandered around the garden together. 'Smell that magnolia, Jock, isn't it heavenly? Doesn't it make you glad to be alive?'

Winston frowned when they came to the water garden.

'Some of the fish seem to be missing.'

Tiger, who was fast getting used to being called Jock, had liver for his dinner in the banqueting room. The dinner guests in their evening suits admired him.

'He really is a beautiful animal – and he just turned up one day, you say?'

'Yes,' Winston said. 'Completely out of the blue. Like Will-o'-the Wisp.'

But like Will-o'-the Wisp, a few days later Tiger was gone.

Chapter 11

Charlie had more trouble than Robert or Lucy getting used to farm life – mainly due to his being terrified of the Red Ruby Devon cows that he was convinced were waiting to eat him as soon as he turned his back on them.

'They look so hungry,' he said to Lucy.

Lucy pointed out that this wasn't true, as all the animals on Mr Foster's farm were very well fed.

And then she explained to Charlie for the tenth time that cows only ate grass. Charlie still looked doubtful. What if they got bored of eating grass and decided they would rather have something more . . . boyish?

The cows looked to Charlie as though they could easily eat a small boy or two for breakfast. And as for the milk that came out of the cows' udders – what a shock it had been the first time he'd seen where milk actually came from: from inside cows! He'd gone right off the taste of it after seeing this, and had asked Mrs Foster for water with his breakfast instead.

Charlie wasn't as easy to look after as either Robert or Lucy, and more than once Mr and Mrs Foster quietly wondered if they'd done the wise thing by agreeing to take him home with them. But Lucy had asked so nicely and Charlie had looked like such a desperate little thing.

When Charlie had had an accident in his bed for the tenth time, Mrs Foster was about to have some firm words with him when she found him sobbing his little heart out, and her own heart melted.

'What is it, Charlie, what's wrong?' she asked him.

Charlie had snot and tears running down his face that he wiped away with his slightly dirty hand, leaving a grey smear across his features. Only Charlie could make such a mess of himself.

'Are you hurt?' she said.

Charlie shook his head. He couldn't speak because he'd got himself into too much of a state. He made hiccupping sounds when he tried to talk.

'So what is it?' Mrs Foster asked him, when he seemed to have calmed down a little.

'I–I–hic . . .'

'Yes?'

'Want my mum.' Charlie managed before dissolving into floods of tears once again.

Mrs Foster hugged him to her, his little wet face pressing into her. She patted his back and let him cry himself out. Amidst the sobs she managed to decipher that it wasn't just that he was missing his mother terribly that was the problem, but that she didn't know where he was, and he didn't know how she was supposed to find him, or how he was going to find his way home 'when Mr Hitter stops vading'.

Charlie's sobs gradually decreased enough for Mrs Foster to start to sort out the muddle he'd got himself into.

'Now,' she said. 'I think it's time you wrote to your mother and told her where you are, don't you?'

'Can't write,' Charlie admitted.

'Then why don't you tell me what you want to say and I'll write it for you, and you can draw her a nice picture, and later on we'll take it to the post office and send it off to London. All right?'

Charlie nodded and managed to smile through his tears. Mrs Foster's suggestion was perfect. But then Charlie's face started to crumple back into misery.

'I don't know my address,' he cried.

'Yes you do,' Mrs Foster said.

'Do I?' Charlie looked surprised.

'Yes,' Mrs Foster told him, and she pointed to his name and address, which were written on the inside of his suitcase.

Charlie frowned when he looked at where she pointed.

'Charlie, can you read your name?' Mrs Foster asked him.

Charlie shook his head.

Mrs Foster pressed her lips together. Charlie's education so far had been sadly lacking. What was the school thinking? She decided there and then that she and Charlie would spend some time together each day learning to read, and by the time 'Mr Hitter stopped vading' and Charlie went home he'd be able to at least read and write his own name.

When Robert and Lucy visited their gran the next day, Charlie went with them.

'I'm Charlie Wilkes,' he said, wiping his fingers on his short trousers and then holding out his hand politely.

'Indeed,' Beatrice said, but she didn't shake his hand. 'And what have I done today to earn the honour of my grandchildren's presence?'

She picked up a shovel and started digging a hole a few feet away from one she'd already dug.

'We thought it'd be better if we stayed with the Fosters. Much less work for you,' Robert said, trying to ease the awkwardness.

Beatrice pulled a face. 'If you don't like my company . . .'

'It wasn't that, truly, Gran,' Lucy said quickly, trying to make peace. 'We'll still come and see you – every day if you like.'

But Beatrice didn't look pleased with that idea either. Charlie thought of his mum saying, 'There's no pleasing some people,' and couldn't help smiling.

'I'm much too busy to have you children under my feet all the time,' the old lady said.

'Digging holes?' Charlie asked.

'We could help,' Robert said, nudging Charlie to be quiet.

'You can come once a week, on Sunday, after I've been to church. That will be more than enough. Make it in the afternoon because you can't expect me to make you luncheon.'

'Do I have to come too?' Charlie asked her. He really hoped that he didn't, although he would if he had to.

Beatrice gave him a look that told him his presence would definitely not be required. Charlie only just managed to hold in a cheer at this news. He didn't like the way Beatrice stared at him with her beady, birdlike eyes.

'She's not even like our gran any more,' Lucy said to Robert when they were alone later. 'I used to love coming here, but now she's so . . . so . . .'

'Unwelcoming?'

'Yes – and what's with all the digging?'

Chapter 12

Autumn crept in as the animals crossed the rolling
hills and wooded valleys of the Kent countryside.
Late one afternoon they were passing through an
apple orchard when three saddleback pigs came
running at them.

Tiger raced up into the branches of the nearest
apple tree – where he batted his paw and hissed at
the pigs. Rose growled deep in her throat as the pigs
surrounded them. Buster lay down, in a submissive
pose.

Then one of the pigs rolled over beside Buster just
like another dog might have done. Buster joined in
the pig game and rolled on his back with his four
legs waving in the air. Rose wagged her tail. Tiger
remained in the tree, where he washed himself from
tail to paws.

With a squeal the pigs started to play chase. The
dogs joined in and were much faster, but it didn't
matter as they raced round the orchard.

Finally, tired and hot, they all waded into the

muddy pond to cool off. Buster and Rose emerged with their coats dripping in mud.

Buster sat and watched as the pigs started to chomp on the windfall apples. He whined with hunger. There were apples everywhere.

Buster crunched on one and found he liked it. He tried a second one.

One apple was easy, two was no problem, but number three didn't taste as good as the first two, so he only had a bite before dropping it for one of the pigs to snuffle up.

By the sixth apple – and really he hadn't eaten much of the last three and the pigs had had much more than him – Buster was heartily sick of apples and had a stomach ache.

As the sun set, Rose whined and urged them onwards. But Buster had eaten far too many apples for a little dog and started to be sick.

Rose found a pigsty for them to sleep in; Tiger sat on top of the corrugated iron shed. But during the night it started to rain and the cat crept inside the sty to curl up with the dogs.

Every morning Lucy woke up missing her mum and her dad and the pets. Her mother and father wrote to her whenever they could, but Buster, Rose and Tiger couldn't do that. All she could do was wait and hope that today would be the day that a letter from Mrs Harris arrived to tell her how they were.

And every morning, so far, she'd been disappointed.

There was no electricity or gas in the longhouse and all the cooking had to be done in a coal-fired oven with two hot plates at the top. After breakfast Lucy helped Mrs Foster make the pasties the children took to school for their lunch.

'My mum taught me how to make these,' Mrs Foster told Lucy as she prepared the ingredients. 'And I expect her mother taught her and her mother before her taught her.'

'And now you're teaching me,' Lucy smiled.

'There's always been bad blood between Devon and Cornwall over who invented the pasty,' Mrs Foster said, as she started to work the butter, flour and water together in a bowl.

Just like the bad blood between the locals and evacuees, thought Lucy – *with me and Robert in the middle.* School hadn't been getting any better for her and it seemed to be just as bad for Robert.

She'd tried to get him to talk about it, but he wouldn't. All he'd say was that it wouldn't be for long and it wasn't too bad, but she was sure he was lying. He looked totally miserable as they trudged down the country lanes on their way to school that morning.

'Don't eat that yet, Charlie.'

Charlie put the pasty he was finding hard to resist back in his bag.

'What lessons have you got today?' Lucy asked Robert, as they approached the school gates.

Robert looked vague and said he didn't know, which just made Lucy even more sure that there was something wrong at school. In London Robert was top of his class in most subjects and he always knew what lessons he'd be having each day.

When they got to school Lucy and Robert and Charlie stayed together in the playground. At least they had each other.

'See you later,' Robert said, as the handbell was rung for lessons to begin.

At breaktime the girl Lucy privately called 'Pincher Jane' pushed her.

'Teacher's pet!'

And something in Lucy snapped.

'Am not!'

She pushed the girl back.

Pincher Jane pulled Lucy's hair. She kicked out, then tried to scratch Lucy's face but missed. Shielding her face with her arms, Lucy scored a direct hit with her scratch, leaving marks all down Pincher Jane's face.

Pincher Jane screamed and the London school's headmaster, Mr Faber, came over, swishing his cane. The two girls quickly backed away from each other.

'What's going on?' he demanded to know.

'Nothing,' they both mumbled.

'What happened to your face?'

'Fell,' Pincher Jane told him, looking daggers at Lucy.

The bell rang, but Lucy was sure it wasn't over yet. She was glad she had Robert to walk home with that day, especially when she saw Pincher Jane and some of her cronies loitering at the school gates.

'Hurry up, Charlie,' Lucy told him.

Charlie wasn't sure why they had to walk so fast and he didn't like it much.

Lucy ran over to the cow field as soon as they got back from school. Of all the animals on the farm the cows were Lucy's favourites. And of all the cows her favourite was Daisy.

Some people thought cows were stupid, but Lucy knew they were wrong. Cows were just as intelligent as horses, or at least the Red Ruby Devon cows, which were the only ones she'd spent any time with, were.

When Lucy looked into Daisy's eyes she could see that Daisy was studying her just as much as she was studying Daisy.

It seemed only natural to confide in her and she told Daisy all about how much she was missing Tiger, Rose and Buster and how much she hated Pincher Jane.

'I tried not to fight her, I really did, but what choice did I have?'

'None,' a voice said, and Lucy almost jumped out of her skin because she hadn't realized he was there.

Robert stroked Daisy. 'I hate it too. I try to keep out of Mr Faber's way because he's mean, Lucy, really mean.'

In London Mr Faber had been the headmaster of the evacuee school, but in Devon he had to teach a class.

'He'll get a bee in his bonnet about a kid – usually Benson, he's not too bright – and he'll make an example of him all day, making him sit in the corner when he gets his work wrong.

'And then there's this other boy, Harley; he's no good at sports, but Faber will have him hanging from a rope in the hall for hours, too terrified to go up or down. And if you try to say something . . . well! I did once and he made me climb that rope too; luckily the caretaker came in to arrange the chairs for lunchtime, otherwise I don't know how long he'd have made me stay up there.'

'What about the girls?' Lucy asked him. 'What's he like to them?'

'Not as bad as to the boys. But there's a few of them he's got it in for.

'You only see him in the playground. I know he's bad there too, but he's nowhere near as nasty as when he closes that classroom door. It's like he really enjoys hurting the kids. He makes Sloggings seem like an angel.'

'So what are we going to do?' Lucy said.

'Keep our heads down.'

Lucy nodded.

'And stay out of trouble like we promised Dad,' he added pointedly.

Lucy grinned.

'Don't worry, it'll all be over soon and we can go back to London.'

'But will it – will it really all be over soon?' Lucy wasn't so sure. 'I haven't heard anything from Mrs Harris about the pets, even though I've written to her twice now.'

'I'm sure they're fine,' Robert said, although his voice didn't sound quite convinced. He hadn't heard anything from Michael about the pets either.

Michael was too young to be officially part of NARPAC, so he manned the tea urn at the back of the meeting hall, listening as a vet instructed their North London NARPAC group on how to give first aid to an injured animal.

'The first thing to remember is that an injured pet is a frightened beast,' the vet told them. 'A dog that may usually not say boo to a goose can do a lot more than that when it's in pain. That's why you should always use a grasper.' He held up a long pole with a noose on the end of it. 'Or put a muzzle on the animal before treating it. Otherwise it could end up being you that gets injured when the creature bites you.'

There was polite laughter at this, but many people

knew from experience that what the vet said was true; it was a serious point.

'If it's safe to approach and the dog is bleeding, the best thing to do is hold a towel, or something similar, to the wound and press on it to stop the blood flow.'

'What if it's got rabies?' asked one of their group. 'How could we tell?'

Some bright spark let out a werewolf howl.

'Rabies has three stages recognized in dogs,' the vet told them. The room went completely silent as everyone listened. 'The period between infection and symptoms can vary, but once symptoms show there is a one- to three-day period of behaviour change; this is followed by what we call the excitative stage . . .'

Everyone knew what that meant – a crazed animal given to biting anything that was near.

'And then the third stage is marked by rear limb paralysis, drooling, difficulty swallowing and, ultimately, death.'

'What about in people, what would happen to us if we got it? Would we start biting others?' a lady asked the vet.

'The first symptom is feeling like you have the flu, but this can be a long while after you've been bitten . . .'

'So we'd need to be bitten?'

'Yes. And although you probably wouldn't start

biting people, it does affect the brain, resulting in delirium.'

'How long from symptoms showing till death?' someone else asked.

'Two to ten days.'

'Would it be possible to mistake a dog having a seizure for one with rabies?'

'I wouldn't have thought so,' the vet said. But everyone was still worried and talked during the tea break about the risk of meeting a dog with rabies. Maybe people hadn't been so foolish in having their pets put down. If Hitler infected their animals with rabies . . . it hardly bore thinking about. But it wasn't just pets that were at risk. It was farm animals too. Any mammal could get it and pass it on to any other animal.

When they got home from the meeting, Michael's dad got out a pair of thick leather gloves and gave them to Michael. 'Make sure you put these on before treating any stray animal you don't know,' he said.

'But, Dad . . .'

'Promise me.'

Michael promised and then went to check that all the animals' water bowls were full. They'd already taken in more animals than their small house could really contain, but there were still hundreds of once-loved pets now wandering the city, lost and unwanted. And there were recently-born puppies and kittens too – what chance did they have? Michael was so angry at it all.

The animal shelters were bursting with strays. Those that had identity tags were safe while their owners were sought. But far more were without tags and couldn't be identified and so were virtually condemned to death. No one was looking to take on a new pet during the war.

Michael wished that there was more he could do. If he could have, he would have saved every one of them. They'd done nothing to deserve their fate.

Chapter 13

As the days went by, and the leaves on the trees in the Sussex countryside turned from green to orange and red, Rose, Buster and Tiger became a highly successful hunting team. Rose and Buster chased the rabbits, Buster flushing them out of their burrows, or Rose coming from one side and Buster from the other to herd them towards Tiger, who was ready, waiting to pounce.

Squirrels, however, were not so easy to catch.

Sometimes it seemed to Buster that the squirrels were taunting them, waiting till the animals were almost upon them and then racing up a tree to safety.

But one day the squirrels had a shock when Buster, determined to finally catch one and unexpectedly finding a tree with a branch that was wide enough and low enough for a small dog to race up, ran after the squirrel. He soon found himself further up a tree than he'd ever been before, and looking down at Rose on the ground below him.

Buster's descent – minus the squirrel, which ran up another branch and then leapt to the next tree – was much slower than his ascent. His little body trembled as he inched his way down, tummy pressed into the bark for reassurance.

The experience didn't put him off chasing squirrels though, not in the slightest. Luckily, trees with squirrels in them and branches low enough for a small dog to run up were few and far between.

Although Lucy had every intention of following Robert's advice to keep her head down, Pincher Jane had no intention of making that easy for her. She and some of her cronies were waiting for Lucy when they got to school.

'Go to your class, Charlie,' Robert told him.

'But . . .'

'Now.'

Pincher Jane's face was very close to Lucy's. 'Look what you did,' she said, pointing at the scratch marks.

Robert tried to mediate. 'Hang on, there's no need for this. It was half a dozen of one . . .'

'I'm sorry,' Lucy said, but Pincher Jane didn't want apologies. She launched herself at Lucy like a wildcat and Lucy had no choice but to try and defend herself, with Robert trying to pull them apart and a growing crowd of onlookers gathering.

'What's all this?' Mr Faber roared, swishing his cane. The crowd parted to let him through. 'You two again,' he said to Pincher Jane and Lucy. 'And Mr Edwards in the thick of it. I might have known. Hold out your hand.'

'But he didn't do anything!' Lucy cried, horrified.

'Now.'

Robert held out his right hand and Mr Faber struck it with the cane, and then did the same to his left. Lucy and Pincher Jane looked at each other, dreading what was to come. Pincher Jane had tears in her eyes.

'Now let that be a lesson to you.'

They waited for Mr Faber to cane them too, but the handbell started to ring and Mr Faber told them to go to class.

All day long, Lucy worried that Mr Faber would send for her. But he didn't.

Robert sat at the back of his classroom, his hands smarting, hating Mr Faber and the injustice of being caned for trying to make peace and prevent a fight from breaking out.

He wished he was back in London with Michael and his other friends. Later he wrote another letter to Michael on the back of his piece of precious art paper while he was supposed to be copying a still life of some rotten-looking apples. *Mr Faber and Hitler would probably be the best of friends if they met each other*, he wrote. He asked Michael how Buster, Tiger and Rose were getting on and if he'd been able to visit them like he'd said he would, or if he'd been too busy helping his father with his NARPAC work. Robert wished he was old enough to help his own dad on his reconnaissance missions. He missed him badly.

At the airbase Maisy, the WAAF girl, always said the same thing when she saw the planes off, after checking the crew and flight destination on her clipboard. It was part of a standing joke:

'Bring it back in one piece.'

Officer Roger Fletcher hated the two pigeons they took on board with them every flight. 'They're flying rats, that's what they are,' he'd say.

The pigeon wrangler, Jim, didn't approve of Officer Fletcher's attitude and was looking forward to the day, in a couple of weeks' time, when Roger went off to do his pilot's training. He hoped the new man the Air Ministry Pigeon Section was sending had a better attitude to the birds.

'You won't be calling them flying rats when you need them,' Jim said. He'd tried to explain to Roger how homing pigeons were special; how, once they had understood that their home was their home, they knew with some amazing instinct how to get back to it. And as the airfield was now their home, to the airfield they would always return.

But try as Jim might, Roger was not impressed. 'I don't like the way they flap their wings or the noise they make.' Jim shook his head.

When Roger's replacement arrived two weeks later, Jim was not disappointed.

Officer Cadet Joe Lawson might have been only eighteen, but he was more than just a pigeon fancier – he seemed to have an appreciation for all animals. Jim and William Edwards laughed as Joe told how he'd recently shared a train compartment and his sandwiches with three animals – two dogs and a cat.

'And they were some of the finest travelling companions I've known, let me tell you.'

Joe's story made Mr Edwards think about his pets at home, and he told Joe and Jim about Buster's antics. He missed Buster and he missed his family. The men at the base never talked about feeling homesick, but just about everyone was.

Jim took them over to see his latest fledgling pigeons. They had wispy downy yellow feathers on their heads and necks and grey-feather wings. Their beaks seemed long in proportion to an adult pigeon's beak.

Mr Edwards thought they had the look of a young heron about them.

'Aren't they beauties?' Jim said proudly.

And although neither Mr Edwards nor Joe would, if they'd been honest, have called the young pigeons beautiful, they both agreed with him.

'That's my favourite,' Jim said, pointing to one at the back. 'I've called her Lily, after my youngest daughter.'

They turned at the sound of a plane taking off – another reconnaissance plane on its way over to France. They all watched until it disappeared.

Sometimes it seemed to Michael that he was the only one of his age left in the whole of London.

His father had forbidden him from going with him again to the death field after he'd thrown up at the animal cremation fire. It had been the terrible scent in the air, the smell of death, that had first turned his stomach, before they'd even reached the field proper.

But worse was to come as he saw the large bonfire that had been piled high in the field, with pets that had been put down being burnt on it.

'Why?' Michael had gasped in horrified disbelief.

The animals had done nothing to deserve their deaths. Nothing at all.

After that day Michael would look at the pets being taken to be slaughtered and one would wag its tail, or look at him with innocent trusting eyes, or a cat would purr, totally unaware that its life was about to be over. When this happened, it was all Michael could do not to cry. It was all just so wrong. Then there were the pets that hadn't been taken to the animal shelters. The ones that had been abandoned and left to wander the streets and fend for themselves. In some ways that was even worse. What chance would those animals have? And it was only going to get worse as autumn and then winter drew in.

How could pet owners leave their animals to turn feral and most likely end up starving to death?

Michael turned these questions over and over in his mind.

His main NARPAC jobs were to take messages and bring in stray animals – but only those that were no danger to him.

'Don't even attempt to approach a dog you don't like the look of,' his father warned him. 'And if it looks diseased, leave well alone.'

It wasn't enough. He wanted to do more.

Michael found the empty basement by accident. It was in one of the many buildings that had been abandoned, as people left London for their barracks or for the safety of the countryside.

He was following a stray cat that, a glimpse had told him, had recently given birth and surely needed medical attention.

He was just in time to see it squeeze through a hole in a fence. Michael followed despite his father's warnings.

He was surprised to find himself in a large over-grown garden that was totally enclosed.

The cat was just ahead of him.

Michael crouched down so he'd be less frightening.

'Here, girl,' he called.

The cat took a step towards him, wary but curious. 'That's it – come on.'

The cat moved a little closer and Michael was sure she was going to come to him when there was a faint mewling sound and she skittered away. Michael jumped up and ran after the cat, and was just in time to see her disappear down an open basement trap-door.

After descending the steps into the basement Michael could see the cat over in the corner with her four kittens: one ginger tom that reminded Michael a little of Tiger, and three black-and-whites.

He knew he should report this so that the cat and her kittens could be moved to one of the animal shelters. That was the procedure he was supposed to follow. But the animal shelters were so full and had no choice but to put more and more animals down. The cat and her kittens wouldn't stand a chance there. The basement was dry and safe. All they needed was some food and water and they could stay here until the kittens were stronger.

And so it turned out that the cat and her kittens were the first residents of Michael's unofficial animal rescue centre.

Chapter 14

Days blended into each other and began to be almost indistinguishable one from the next, just like the forest areas the pets went through. But some woodland areas, although they looked the same to the animals' eyes, had signs that said 'Private' and 'No Trespassing'. And it was in one of these woodlands, as Rose and Buster chased a rabbit and Tiger waited to pounce, that Rose suddenly let out a yelp of pain.

The gamekeeper had laid thin wire snares to catch rabbits and foxes, and one of these had caught Rose's right fore paw.

The more she struggled to free her trapped leg, the tighter the snare became. The other two watched helplessly as Rose frantically tried to break free.

Tiger raced up a tree and Buster ran to hide in a bush at the sound of rustling. The gamekeeper was coming!

The man held a gun and had a string of dead rabbits over his shoulder. The rabbits had not been as fortunate as Rose: having put their heads in the snares rather than their paws, they'd had no chance of escape, the snares tightening cruelly round their necks as they struggled. Even if they managed to survive until the gamekeeper came, he killed them.

Rose went dead still as the gamekeeper approached, smelling the blood on the man, sensing the danger that she was in.

'What have we here, then?' he said, and he put the dead rabbits on the ground so he could take a better look at Rose. He kept the rifle with him though. If she turned out to be an aggressive dog or was too badly injured from trying to break free from the snare, he would have no second thoughts about shooting her.

The snare was designed so that it tightened as the terrified animal struggled, but released once it stopped struggling. As Rose lay still the snare relaxed a little.

As the gamekeeper crouched down to take a look at Rose, putting his rifle on the ground, Tiger crept down the tree. His plan was to help himself to one of the rabbits, but as there were six tied together it was a lot for him to carry. Buster couldn't resist the smell of fresh meat and came out of the bush. His small, sharp teeth clamped round the dead head of the first animal.

The gamekeeper looked round to find his rabbits gone.

'Hey!' he yelled and he picked up his gun, as Rose gave her paw a sudden, sharp tug, freeing it from the snare. She was up in a second and running after the other two, even though her paw was cut and in agony.

The gamekeeper thumped through the woodland in pursuit of his missing rabbits, swearing at whatever it was that had taken them. He suspected a fox. It was hard to tell in the dense woodland.

The animals slipped quietly away and once the sounds of the angry man had stopped, Rose joined the other two for a rabbit feast.

But the wire snare had cut deep into her flesh and that night Rose's sleep was troubled and fitful. Buster and Tiger stayed close as the collie whimpered and flinched in her sleep.

The next morning Rose staggered to her feet and limped on, although pain thudded through her thin body with every step she took, and an involuntary cry of agony escaped from her panting mouth every now and again.

Soon their travel pace became painfully slow as Rose dragged herself onward, refusing to be defeated. Buster and Tiger brought her food to save her needing to hunt. But the pain soon became so bad that she barely ate. Buster whined and nudged part of a rabbit over to her, but Rose sighed and turned her head away.

It was twilight when the animals stopped to drink at a canal near Loxwood in West Sussex. Here Rose finally lay down and closed her eyes. Buster and Tiger waited, but she didn't open them again. The animals instinctively kept as hidden as possible, especially when they slept, for safety's sake; but Rose was fast asleep right out in the open. Buster barked at her, but she didn't stir. He barked again and danced around her and nuzzled her with his head, but she still didn't move.

Suddenly something much bigger than a duck or a swan or a deer or any other animal they'd seen close to the water before was heading towards them.

Buster was desperate and tried to wake Rose by licking her face. She shouldn't be lying there. She'd be seen. Buster and Tiger fled as the huge horse came closer – but not too far. They crouched low in the bushes and watched.

The blue roan mare was fourteen hands high and tethered to a barge that she was towing. The mare stopped beside Rose and nuzzled her with her giant head. She seemed to have no inclination to move past the collie, but no intention of harming her either.

'Come on, Bluebell, get a move on there,' a voice from the barge called out.

But Bluebell stayed by Rose's side. She tried gently nuzzling Rose again, but the dog didn't stir.

'Go and see what's up with her, Jack.'

A boy hopped off the barge and on to the river-bank to see what Bluebell had stopped for. 'What's wrong, girl?'

Buster and Tiger watched him from their hiding place.

Jack saw Rose lying on the towpath and knelt down beside her.

Rose raised her head a little to look at the boy, but it was a supreme effort for her.

'It's all right, you lie back down again. You'll be all right.' But as Jack spoke he was looking at Rose's injured paw and frowning. 'Grandad!'

'What is it now?'

'Come quick.'

Jack's grandad, the bargee, came off the boat. He bent down to look at Rose. 'What have we got here, then?'

'Will she be all right?' Jack asked him. It was only two months since his old dog, Ben, had gone to sleep and not woken up the next morning. The pain of losing his best friend was still raw.

Alfred never lied to his grandson. 'It don't look good. That paw's infected bad.'

'We've got to help her,' Jack said. They couldn't just leave the dog here to die.

Alfred nodded. He could see Rose's ribs through her fur. A good meal or three wouldn't do her any harm. But that paw. That paw didn't look good. He wasn't sure if he could even save that leg of hers. He lifted Rose's leg to see how far the infection from her wound had spread.

Rose whimpered.

'Bring her on board.'

'It's all right, I won't hurt you, girl,' Jack said, as he lifted Rose into his arms and carried her on board the barge.

Inside was cramped and cosy. The barge's small cooking range was in the rear of the cabin. It was fired by coal and had rails round the top to stop pans and the kettle from falling off. Alfred had been cooking Bluebell some bran mash to which he'd just added some grated carrot and molasses.

'Put her on the bed.'

Jack lay Rose gently down on the narrow bottom bunk bed. At least she'd be warmer and safer in here than outside on the towpath.

The dog was very weak and Alfred wasn't even completely sure that she'd make it through the night.

'She'll be all right, won't she?' Jack said anxiously.

Alfred sighed. Sometimes it was hard never lying to the boy. 'It's hard to say. Willpower will get her through if anything can. It all depends on how strong her will to live is.'

'It's strong, Grandad, I know it is.'

Outside Bluebell whinnied.

'You take her food to her.'

Jack hesitated, not wanting to leave the dog.

'Go on now.'

Jack came on to the towpath with a bucket of food for Bluebell.

'There you go, girl.' He released the mare from her harness and rubbed her down, talking to her all the time.

'Well spotted there, Bluebell. Many a barge horse would have gone straight on, but not you, girl, aye? Not you.'

He blew softly at Bluebell's nose and Bluebell blew back. Then Jack went back on to the barge as twilight turned to night.

Outside Buster and Tiger watched and waited for Rose to come back to them. They waited and watched and watched and waited, and finally fell asleep in the bush where they'd hidden.

The next morning Rose managed to drink some water and eat a little mashed chicken. As Alfred had suspected, the wound on her paw had become infected. He showed Jack how to make a poultice for it and later he lanced the wound to remove the pus.

'I'm sorry, girl,' Alfred said, as Rose whimpered and tried to pull her paw away. 'But it has to be done.'

'What shall we call her?' Jack said.

'Dog'll do.'

But that wasn't good enough for Jack. 'Gypsy, I think we should call her Gypsy.'

For most of the rest of the day Rose slept on Jack's bed. Outside Buster and Tiger waited. They were hungry too, although Buster wasn't quite as hungry as Tiger, as he'd finished off what was left in Bluebell's mash bucket.

Later in the day Tiger disappeared after a large water rat and came back stuffed full and quite ready to go back to sleep while they continued to wait for Rose.

The next morning Bluebell was re-tethered to the barge and it continued on its slow watery journey to the sea. Buster and Tiger followed the barge, at the side of the towpath, unseen.

Chapter 15

Robert had always enjoyed working the sheep with Rose and his grandfather, when his grandfather had been alive. Now one of the things he most enjoyed about living on the farm was helping Mr Foster with his sheep.

Rose and his grandfather had had such a close bond that it was almost as though she knew what he was going to say before he said it. Mr Foster was trying to train his young sheepdog, Molly, but she didn't seem to have the potential to grow into the exceptional sheepdog that Rose had been.

'If I'd have known your grandmother was going to send Rose to London, I would have offered to buy Rose off her,' Mr Foster said. He hadn't been pleased when he'd heard that Rose was now a family pet.

Robert tried to explain that Rose was happy, but Mr Foster shook his head.

'Sheepdogs have a natural instinct to herd, it's in their blood . . .'

Robert nodded, smiling to himself. He'd seen Rose trying unsuccessfully to herd Buster and Tiger. They'd been much less cooperative than the sheep were. Buster would go where she wanted him to – sometimes – but Tiger was impossible to steer anywhere and would hiss at Rose to warn her off.

'But we love Rose,' Lucy said later, when Robert told her Mr Foster didn't think Rose should be a family pet. 'We're always playing with her and we take very good care of her.'

Mr Foster came over to the table, drying his hands.

'I don't doubt that you do, Lucy. Not for one minute. I can see what caring children you are. But the thing is, people who have pet collies don't always realize how strong that herding instinct is within them. A collie that can't herd . . .'

Mrs Foster put Mr Foster's dinner down in front of him. 'Thanks, love.'

'What about a collie that can't herd?' Robert asked him.

Mr Foster cut into his steak and kidney pie. 'It's like a greyhound that can't run or a bird that can't fly,' he said. 'What you've got is a very unhappy animal.'

A week of good food and resting her paw had done wonders for Rose. She was almost unrecognizable as the bedraggled creature Bluebell had found and Jack had carried on to the barge.

For the first few days she'd been unable to do more than lie on Jack's bed and sleep and eat, but the poultice had helped to heal the infection, and then Alfred wrapped a bandage round Rose's paw and used part of a sack as a slipper over the bandage to keep it clean, and Rose was free to wander the barge – cramped and narrow as it was.

The weather had turned warm and bright for October, and Rose liked to sit on the bow of the barge and see where they were heading next.

Bluebell trundled along on the riverbank's towpath, pulling the coal-laden barge behind her.

Jack would often sit on the bow with Rose – or Gypsy, as he called her – just as he'd done with Ben. He liked having her with them. She was good company.

'Bet you'd have so much to tell me if you could only speak, Gypsy,' Jack told Rose, as a mother duck and her six ducklings swam past.

Buster and Tiger followed along behind. The barge wasn't hard to keep in sight and was easy to find after they came back from foraging for food. The canal went on relentlessly wending its way to the sea, taking the barge and the animals with it.

Robert and Lucy's position at the village school hadn't got any better after Robert's caning. But the trouble between Lucy and Pincher Jane had quietened down a little. Pincher Jane still looked daggers at Lucy, but she kept her distance.

Charlie didn't help himself much by saying at every opportunity how much he liked staying with Mr and Mrs Foster, and how great Robert was and how strong he was and how if anyone thought they could beat Charlie up they'd have to go through Robert first.

Unfortunately, one of the people he told this to was the little brother of the leader of the biggest boy-group of evacuees. The kid told his big brother Gopher that Charlie had said Robert could take him, any day, which wasn't exactly what Charlie had said, but which enraged Gopher all the same.

It might have helped if Charlie had told Robert what he'd said, but he didn't think of it – so Robert had no warning when Gopher confronted him outside school the next morning.

'So you think you can take me?' said Gopher.

'What? No – I . . .'

But Gopher was too worked up to listen, and he swung at Robert with a right hook that Robert only narrowly managed to avoid by ducking.

A crowd formed around the boys, shouting: 'Fight, fight, fight!'

Gopher's left arm took a swing and without even thinking Robert dodged and blocked him and punched him hard in the stomach.

Gopher doubled over in pain, then spun round and tried to backhand Robert in the face, but Robert blocked it and then drove his fist up, smashing Gopher's head back.

Gopher staggered, as Mr Faber came storming up, waving his cane as usual like an extension of his arm.

'What's going on?'

'It was his fault,' Gopher gasped, pointing at Robert. 'He started it.'

The others in Gopher's gang chorused in agreement. 'Yes – he started it, sir.'

'Troublemaker.'

'No he didn't,' Lucy shouted. 'He didn't do anything!'

'Like the last time he was caught fighting, I presume?' Mr Faber said.

'Yes,' Lucy said, but even as she spoke the word she knew she wasn't helping.

'Hold out your hand.'

'Wait!' Robert tried to protest, but he could see in Mr Faber's face that he didn't believe him. Or maybe he just wanted to make an example of somebody, anybody, as quickly as possible.

Gopher and his gang smirked.

Robert heard the swish of the cane before he felt the sharp crack as it struck his upturned palm, sending waves of pain up through his arm.

'Other hand,' Mr Faber said, and he brought the cane down even harder this time, almost knocking Robert to the ground with the force of it. 'Now let that be a lesson to you.' His face was so close to Robert's that Robert could smell his sour breath.

For the rest of that day Robert sat at the back of the classroom hating Mr Faber while his hands burned. It was worse than last time; his hands still throbbed as he walked home with Lucy and Charlie. Lucy kept glancing over at him, worried. Charlie started snivelling.

'What's the matter with you?' Lucy said. 'You're not the one who got caned.'

'I – I – I'm sorry,' Charlie told Robert.

'Sorry for what?' Robert said, and the whole story came out.

'You shouldn't go round making things up,' Lucy said. She was angry with Charlie on Robert's behalf.

Robert looked as though he couldn't quite believe the story that was coming out of Charlie's mouth.

'But you would protect me, wouldn't you, Robert?' Charlie said. He didn't want that part to have been a lie.

And for the first time in a long time Robert found himself laughing, and the sting in his hands wasn't quite so bad any more.

'Of course I would!' he said.

Charlie looked relieved and then he looked surprised. 'What's your gran doing in there?' he suddenly asked.

Robert looked over to where Charlie was pointing. Their gran was sitting on a haystack next to a scarecrow in the middle of the opposite field.

Lucy and Robert ran towards her.

'Hey, wait for me,' Charlie shouted, and ran after them as fast as his much shorter legs could go.

'Gran, are you all right?' Robert said. What was she doing here? She looked frozen to the bone. He took off his coat and wrapped it round her thin shoulders.

Lucy took her gran's hand as Charlie came running up to them.

'What's wrong with her?' he said. He was out of breath from the running.

Beatrice hardly even seemed to know who they were.

'Gran, it's us, Robert and Lucy, your grandchildren,' Lucy said slowly, as if she was speaking to someone who was half asleep.

'And me,' said Charlie. 'Don't forget me. I'm Charlie, missis.' He took Beatrice's other hand and pumped it up and down.

The vigorous handshake seemed to bring Beatrice back to herself a little.

'Lucy?' she said. 'What are you doing here? Why aren't you in London? Where's your mother?'

'Come on, Gran,' Robert said. 'Let's take you home.' He helped her up and she went with them willingly.

They took Beatrice back to her farm and into the farmhouse. It was freezing cold. Lucy set about making a fire.

'Go and see to the chickens,' Robert told Charlie.

'Do I have to?' Charlie said. He wasn't very keen on Mr and Mrs Foster's chickens and didn't expect Robert and Lucy's gran's chickens to be any friendlier.

'Yes, you have to,' Robert said. 'And check that any other animals have been fed. You wouldn't want them to be hungry, would you?'

'No,' Charlie said.

'The chickens probably haven't even had any breakfast yet,' Robert said.

So Charlie went.

Lucy made Gran a cup of sweet tea and Robert found a woollen blanket to wrap round her shoulders.

'Why don't you come back to the Fosters' with us?' Robert said. 'At least you'd be warm there.'

But Beatrice wouldn't hear of it. 'I've slept in my own bed for fifty years. I could never sleep anywhere else,' she said. 'And anyway I've got too much work to do to go lollygagging about.'

'Do you think we should let Mum know?' Lucy said, when Gran wasn't listening.

Robert wasn't sure. 'She'd be so worried.'

Charlie came running in from feeding the chickens. His knee was scraped.

'What happened to you?' Lucy asked him.

He pointed his head in Beatrice's direction. 'Fell down one of the holes.'

At the Fosters' house the wireless had pride of place in the floral-wallpapered living room and once it was on, it was given everyone's full attention. The front room wasn't used much during the week, unless there were special visitors, which there never seemed to be. But every Sunday afternoon Mr and Mrs Foster liked to listen to the 'In Your Garden' programme. Before the war Britain had been able to import much of the food it needed, but now the Ministry of Food wanted people to grow their own.

Charlie liked to show off his arm muscles as the special 'Dig for Victory' song was played. He was sure they must be growing bigger with all the digging he'd been doing since coming to the farm.

When the children finally arrived home from school that day, Mrs Foster announced that she was trying out one of the recipes from last Sunday's show. 'Would you like a drink to go with your dinner?' she asked. She took a jug of something orange from the cool pantry and poured them a glass each.

Robert picked his glass up carefully. He didn't want either Mr or Mrs Foster to know that he'd been caned. He took a sip just as Lucy took one from her glass. They gave each other a look.

'Mmm, delicious,' said Mrs Foster, taking a large swig.

Charlie was suspicious. The drink smelt funny. 'What is it?' he asked.

'Why don't you try it and see,' Mrs Foster said brightly.

But Charlie didn't think he would. 'What's it called?' he asked.

'Carrotade,' Mrs Foster said.

'Carrotade?' Charlie echoed.

Lucy took another sip of her drink, not wanting to upset Mrs Foster by not drinking it.

'It's really not too bad, Charlie,' Lucy said. Although it really was horrible. 'Try some.'

'What's it made of?' Charlie asked.

'It's made from carrots and swede juice,' Mrs Foster admitted, and she forced herself to take another mouthful of the unappetizing concoction. 'It's good for you – and it'll help you see better in the dark.'

When Mr Foster took a large swig from his glass, the face he pulled convinced Charlie that carrotade was another name for poison.

Although Robert did his best to keep his hands hidden, Mr Foster noticed something was wrong.

'What happened to your hands?' he asked.

'Nothing,' Robert started to say.

But Lucy was too incensed not to speak. 'It was so unfair. Mr Faber shouldn't have done it. He didn't cane the one who started it, just Robert.' Tears slipped down her face. 'It was just like last time.'

Mr Foster looked at Robert.

He lowered his eyes and a blush crept across his face. 'I . . . I got the cane for fighting,' Robert said.

'He was innocent!' Lucy protested.

'It was my fault for saying Robert was brave,' Charlie told Mr Foster.

'Eat your dinner,' Mr Foster said.

And Charlie did, even though the mouthfuls were much harder to swallow than normal.

After dinner Mr and Mrs Foster had a whispered chat and then Mr Foster picked up his coat and left the house. He was gone for more than an hour before they heard his truck pull up in the farmyard.

He came in looking grim. Robert knew he couldn't necessarily expect Mr Foster to believe him over a grown-up.

'You won't be going to school for the next few weeks,' Mr Foster said.

Robert didn't know what to say. Part of him wanted to cheer with relief. But part of him was worried. 'Have I been expelled?' he asked.

'No – if there's still no bombs in London, the London school is going back at the end of term and taking their teachers, including your Mr Faber, with them. For now, I need you on the farm.'

Robert nodded, feeling a gigantic surge of relief. 'Thank you.'

As Rose got better, she moved about the barge more, but her favourite place to sit was always the bow.

'You're like our figurehead,' Jack said, and Rose looked at him as if she understood every word.

Sailors had believed for centuries that a figurehead

brought them luck. For Jack the sight of Rose in the bow always made him smile, and as his grandfather said, to be happy was good fortune indeed.

While Rose basked in the sun at the front of the barge, Buster and Tiger trailed along behind. Together the two of them were an excellent hunting team, and water rats and rabbits didn't really stand a chance with Buster flushing them out into Tiger's path and Tiger waiting, ready to pounce.

And then one morning, very early, ten days after she had collapsed, Rose knew it was time to leave the warmth and security of the barge. Jack had reclaimed his own bed and made Rose a bed of her own from some sacking and a blanket on the floor. Before she went, Rose spent a long time watching Jack sleeping. It would be easy to stay with him, to spend her days on the barge watching the riverbank pass by.

Rose slipped out of the cabin and jumped off the barge on to the bank.

Bluebell bent her head to nuzzle her and Rose wagged her tail.

In the cabin Jack woke and saw that Rose wasn't there.

In the bushes Buster and Tiger waited for her. Bluebell whinnied as Rose ran to them.

Buster danced around her with delight when she joined them. Tiger showed a little more restraint and licked his paws, before launching himself at her and circling round and round her, bumping his head against her legs.

From the barge deck Jack watched as the three friends greeted each other.

He kept very quiet and didn't call out or try to stop her, even though more than anything he wanted her to stay. Rose looked back just before the animals disappeared into the woodland and Jack raised his hand in a goodbye.

He knew she wouldn't be back.

'Where's Gypsy?' Alfred asked, when he got up.

Jack told him that Gypsy was gone and what he'd seen.

'Somewhere else she needed to be,' Alfred said, and Jack nodded.

He gave Bluebell her breakfast and rubbed her neck. 'If you hadn't stopped on that towpath when you did, then Gypsy probably wouldn't have survived,' he told her. 'You're a good horse, you are.'

He tethered Bluebell to the barge and Alfred cast off the rope.

'Let's get going, old girl,' Jack said to Bluebell, and they continued on their watery way.

Chapter 16

Michael tried not to bring too many unwanted pets to the basement, but it was so hard to choose who should be allowed in and who should not. He tried to make a decision on whether each animal would be able to survive without his help, but it was virtually impossible to do so: all of them would be better off having regular food and a dry place to sleep.

Every time he went there he knew he'd done the right thing. He'd blocked the fence hole off but left the basement trapdoor open so the animals could come in and out as they liked.

The kittens were stronger now and full of energy. They raced to greet him and see what food he'd brought them.

As well as the kittens and their mother there was an elderly yellow Lab, two puppies of unknown breed, an Old English sheepdog, a Siamese cat, a tabby and three black cats – one of which was blind and tended by the other two. Michael loved them all.

He used his own savings and bought food for them from the butcher's on the High Street and mixed it with biscuits or oats and rice. He'd told no one about the place. But he was facing the very real problem of not having enough money to keep buying food for much longer. He couldn't ask his dad or NARPAC for help, but the animals would need even more food as they got bigger and stronger. He stared around the basement at the collection of animals. What was he going to do when he ran out of money?

Rose sniffed the air, her powerful nose catching the tang of the sea in the distance. The salty smell reminded her of her old home and mornings when the wind drove the smell of the sea up on to the moor where the sheep grazed.

Buster and Tiger followed Rose down to the estuary, their paws growing accustomed to the soft-ness of the yielding wet sand beneath them. Buster was thirsty and drank deeply from the salty water. Tiger took one lap and didn't drink any more, but Buster kept on drinking, only to retch the water back up.

The estuary proved to be a larder of delights, a banquet of crabs and tide-stranded fishes. Buster was the first to spot a crab, and leapt at it, but it scuttled away and dug itself into the sand. He saw another and pounced on that, and this time when the crab tried to bury itself Buster was right behind it, digging too. He barked at the crabs as they tried to scuttle away from him, his little tail going nineteen to the dozen.

Tiger stalked the many wild birds that came to feed on the shrimps, crabs and small fishes. He sent flocks of Brent geese flying up into the sky and away whenever they spotted him.

Rose did not bark at her sea prey; she rarely barked at all, although she too feasted on the seafood. Often she sniffed at the air and seemed to be listening to the wind and the sea – as if it were directing her home.

As they followed the estuary to the sea and got closer to the beach, Buster spotted a creature bobbing in the waves. He raced into the sea and swam in and out of the waves with the seal, chasing the spray. Finally, he grew too cold and had to come in from the water, where he joined the other two on the beach, shivering and exhausted. The seal swam away to find other playmates.

That night they slept by the hull of an old fishing boat and they woke the next morning to find themselves near a harbour. It was early and the fishermen had just come in to shore with their catch.

Tiger was the most brazen of the three pets, and even when he was caught trying to steal some of the catch that the fishermen were selling he was rewarded with a fish head for his efforts.

'Go on then, cat, here you go.'

On the one occasion Buster tried to copy him he was pounced on himself.

'Got you!' said a fisherman, scooping Buster up by the scruff of his neck. Buster twisted and turned, trying to get free, his short legs flailing desperately. But he couldn't get away.

Then Tiger yeowled and hissed at the man and Rose danced around him baring her teeth, growling and barking, and the fisherman dropped Buster in surprise at their ferocity.

Buster landed on his back, but was up in a second and racing across the beach after the other two.

'Dumb animals!' the fisherman said, as the other fishermen around him laughed.

'Better stick to catching fish from now on!' one of them joked.

Always wary, Rose scavenged for food among the fish guts and wastage that was left behind at the harbour. She was more careful to avoid human contact than the other two, and Buster soon chose to copy what she did, checking that there was no one watching him before taking whatever he could find.

The three pets continued on round the coast, scavenging whenever they could, hunting whatever they could and sleeping anywhere they could find that was safe and dry.

Rose and Buster's sensitive ears began to recognize the soft mosquito-like drone that turned into a roar as it came closer. They'd heard it more and more often as they travelled along the South Coast. The animals cowered, and then raced along the beach away from the patrolling RAF planes.

Soon the only people they saw on the beaches were soldiers putting up barbed-wire blockades to turn the beaches into no-go areas.

The soldiers shooed Rose, Buster and Tiger away with shouts and stone-throwing if they saw them.

'Get away from the beach, you stupid animals . . .'

'You'll get yourselves blown to smithereens.'

The pets, not knowing why they were being treated with so much hostility, ran away, leaving the unwelcoming barbed-wire shoreline and heading inland.

Jim was proud of how well he knew his pigeons. Even though most people could never tell the birds apart, Jim knew each pigeon was uniquely different and found them as easy to identify as his own children.

Not only did the pigeons look different from each other, to Jim's knowing eyes, their personalities were also different. Some gobbled up their food like it was the last meal they'd ever have, while others took it at a leisurely pace. They had preferred ways and places to sleep and once a pigeon chose a mate it was its mate for life.

Naturally, knowing his pigeons so well and observing them so acutely, Jim had his favourites, and of all his favourites, his most favourite was Lily. She had a way of tipping her head to one side and looking at him when he spoke to her that made him truly believe that the tiny feathery creature could understand his every word. Not that he said as much to the others on the airbase, of course. They'd think he'd gone loop de loop!

Lily had been born in the loft and successfully completed her training flights. She was fast, although not as fast as Hercules. Hercules was the fastest bird he'd ever had.

Lily was due to make her first flight by plane, a thought that made Jim nervous because of the risk of her being killed or not returning. Because young Joe Lawson knew his pigeons and William Edwards was a good man, Jim chose their Blenheim plane for Lily's first flying trip. It wasn't to be that long a flight. A short reconnaissance trip across the sea.

Joe had the pigeon carriers strapped to him and would attach a message to Lily's leg should anything go wrong. They took two pigeons with them on every trip. Nothing had gone wrong so far and no one was expecting anything to go wrong this time. Along with Lily, Jim had to choose a more experienced pigeon to go on the flight. After some deliberation the pigeon he selected to go with Lily was his fastest bird, Hercules.

'You watch out for her and come back safe, hear?'

He gave both the pigeons some corn and then took them over to the Blenheim.

'Take care of them,' Jim told Joe.

'I will. Don't you worry,' Joe grinned.

Jim watched as the engineer drove the plane out of the hangar and William Edwards and his crew climbed on board.

He was still watching as William took over the controls and drove the plane down the runway and up into the crisp winter sky. He kept watching the plane until it was out of sight, and then he went back to the pigeon loft and brewed himself an extra-strong pot of tea.

In the cramped cockpit William steered the Blenheim towards the South Coast.

It was always freezing inside the plane and today it was even more so, but at least the snow had stopped falling for now and visibility was good. The sky was a vivid blue and clear, with just a few white clouds on the horizon. A perfect day for a reconnaissance sortie.

'Everyone all right back there?' he said into his inner communication headset.

'Yes, sir,' came the crackled reply.

In the back of the plane Joe had Lily and Hercules with him safely in their special pigeon vests that were attached to his parachute harness.

'Up, up and away,' he said to the birds. Lily blinked.

William flew the Blenheim out over the waves in the direction of France. Today's mission seemed much like any other mission – until he saw the Messerschmitt Bf 109 flying towards them. They hadn't been expecting to see one on a routine mission. What was it doing here?

'Guv . . .' the camera operator's voice crackled.

'I see it,' William said into his headset.

The Messerschmitt was heading straight for them at 340 miles an hour and was already dangerously close.

William steered his plane downwards – if the Messerschmitt got a hit at the Blenheim's vulnerable underbelly they'd have no chance of survival.

His quick manoeuvre stopped the German plane from getting under them, but it didn't stop the machine-gun onslaught that followed. The Messerschmitt's fire shot out the horizontal tail-plane and the steering cable was cut through. More gunfire hit the wing and they started hurtling downwards.

'Bail out!' William yelled into his headset. 'Bail out!'

Michael knew he should have told his father about his secret pet rescue place. But days went by and all the time the pet rescue kept growing. Once he'd started, he couldn't turn an animal away. Not when he knew what the alternative would be. He just couldn't.

'What can I get you today?' asked the red-faced butcher on the High Street, where he'd become a regular customer.

Michael showed him the last few coins he had left from his birthday and Christmas money.

'Right.'

The butcher disappeared into the back and came back with a bag of bones. 'Threw in a few sausages and some other bits I can't use.'

'Thank you.' Michael held out his money.

'On the house. Used to have a dog myself when I was a boy – Sailor, I called him, don't know why. That dog followed me everywhere, broke my heart when I lost him.'

'I'm sorry,' Michael said.

The butcher nodded. 'I don't care what anyone says, your lot are doing a good job.'

The bell on the butcher's shop door jingled as Michael left with his meat.

As Michael moved the plank of wood he'd used to block off the gap in the fence and squeezed through the hole with his bag of bones he couldn't help smiling at the butcher's kindness.

But as he approached the basement, he realized something was wrong. Usually there'd be at least one or two animals out in the garden. As he got nearer, he had a horrible feeling that twisted in the pit of his stomach. It was so quiet – much too quiet.

He'd left the basement trapdoor wedged open, but now it was closed. He ran to the basement and pulled open the trapdoor with mounting dread.

'No!'

The pets were all gone. He heard the rattle of a van engine starting up and ran round to the front of the house in time to see the NARPAC van drive off. He ran down the street after it as fast as he could, feeling like his heart was breaking.

'Wait!' he gasped, as it left him behind.

But it didn't stop. It disappeared into the distance, taking his animals with it.

Chapter 17

Now that Robert wasn't attending school any more, he spent his days with Mr Foster, helping on the farm.

Most of all he liked going out on the moorland where Mr Foster grazed his sheep. Often they took Molly with them and Mr Foster taught Robert, successfully, and Molly, with a lot less success, the commands that a shepherd uses with a sheepdog to herd sheep.

Some of the commands Robert remembered from when he used to go out shepherding with his grandfather.

'Come-bye' was used when the shepherd wanted the sheepdog to circle the sheep in a clockwise direction. 'Away to me' was used for anticlockwise.

'Grandad used to whistle,' Robert said, and Mr Foster nodded.

'I'll be using a whistle too if I can ever get her to understand the basic commands,' he said, with a grimace.

The problem with Molly seemed to be that she wasn't really all that interested in the sheep and didn't much mind if they were rounded up or not.

The strong natural herding instinct seemed to be missing in her and she'd much rather spend her time running after the ball that Robert would throw for her. She'd chase after it, her tail wagging constantly, eyes beseeching Robert to throw it again as soon as she'd brought it to him.

'She's just not got the makings of a sheepdog,' Mr Foster said with resignation.

'So what will you do with her?' Robert asked. Animals in the country had to earn their keep. No one had pets in the same way that people in towns did. Most people couldn't afford to. A dog in Devon had to be a working dog, and Molly showed little natural ability for that.

'Nothing, for the moment,' Mr Foster said. 'Not till this war's over. I'm hoping it'll all be done by Christmas and we can get back to normal. Then we'll see.'

Robert was worried for Molly's sake. Who would want to take her on down here?

He spent hours on the moor with Molly, trying to get her to learn how to be a sheepdog. But all she really wanted to do was play with her ball.

As Robert watched Molly make a mess of the simplest of tasks, he couldn't help but compare her to Rose, who'd been so eager and so able to do whatever sheepdog task his grandfather had asked her to.

If only she were here to teach Molly a thing or two! he thought.

The pets awoke to the sounds of gunfire.

After a long day of hunting the day before, Rose, Buster and Tiger had travelled upwards and across country until they came to a clearing with some giant stone structures. Exhausted, their paws tired from walking, they'd settled down beside the strange stones and gone to sleep, watched over by the full moon.

Now, amidst the gunshots, they heard a loud rumbling sound. There was only one thing the animals could do when they saw a huge steel creature hurtling towards them, and that was run.

Sergeant Hooper, who was leading a military training exercise on Salisbury Plain, spotted the Jack Russell from his tank.

'Get that dog!' he told two of his men. They didn't look particularly willing to go after it. 'And don't come back until you do,' he added.

'But, guv . . .'

Sergeant Hooper gave them a look that said he expected obedience, however long it took.

'Yes, sir.'

'The wind's in your favour. Use all the tracking skills you've been taught.'

'Yes, sir.'

Buster, Tiger and Rose gradually outran the terrible steel beasts, and kept on running until they were too exhausted to run any more.

They stopped at a stream for a long, cool drink of water, and the panic was quickly forgotten. It was time for food. In the woods they chased a deer, but it was too fast for them. It disappeared into the bushes and they lost it.

Then Buster got the scent of a rabbit and was after it with terrier determination. Tiger did not choose to go down rabbit holes and Rose was too big. But Buster went straight down the hole – although it was a very tight squeeze. He simply had to get the rabbit and he wouldn't be back until he did.

At the sound of the soldiers coming, Tiger leapt on to a branch of a tree and climbed higher and higher, while Rose lay down in a bush, hidden from view.

Buster was unaware of the men's presence.

'I saw it go this way, I tell you.'

Buster had almost reached the rabbit, could smell it just ahead. But the frightened creature had escaped through one of the warren's many entrances and exits seconds before Buster's head came poking out of it. The dog was grabbed by two strong hands.

'Got you!'

Buster struggled and tried to escape, but the hands held on and wouldn't let him go.

Tiger and Rose looked on, unseen by the soldiers.

Rose crouched down lower as they passed her, out of sight now. And then Rose and Tiger heard the terrible sound of a single gunshot being fired.

Bonfire Night had to be suspended because of the war, of course, but during the day there was a party in the village hall for the school children to celebrate it.

Lucy and Charlie were having a good time until Beatrice turned up in her nightdress, slippers on her feet.

Pincher Jane pointed at Beatrice and laughed scornfully. 'She's mad.'

'Don't say that about my gran!' Lucy told her.

Even if she was beginning to wonder it herself, she didn't want anyone else saying it.

'Must run in the family,' Pincher Jane snickered to her friends. But she didn't say any more when she saw Lucy's glowering face.

'Gran, are you all right?' Lucy asked Beatrice, although it was obvious that she wasn't all right. Not at all.

She guided her to a chair and Lucy got her a cup of tea and some cake. Everyone was staring at her.

Beatrice took a sip of the tea, but she seemed disorientated and not at all sure who Lucy was or where she was.

'Have you seen little Bertie?' she asked. 'I can't

find him, and his father is going to be so angry with me. He dotes on that boy.'

Lucy knew she was talking about Uncle Bertie.

'If you see him, tell him to come home, will you? His dinner is getting cold.'

'I'll tell him,' Lucy said.

They had to get Gran home.

'Come on, Charlie,' said Lucy. 'We've got to go.'

Charlie was not pleased to have to leave the party early.

'When I'm big, I'm going to do whatever I like and not what other people tell me,' he pouted as they left the hall. 'And I'm going to be a soldier. Bang, bang, bang!'

He was very surprised when Beatrice grabbed him by the shoulders and shook him hard.

'No you're not!' she said.

'But . . .'

She shook him again, her thin fingers pinching into his flesh. 'You're not going to war. You can't go to war.'

Lucy tried to help Charlie. 'Gran, you're hurting him,' she said. She tried to pull Beatrice away, but her gran wouldn't let go of Charlie.

'Come on, Gran. Leave him alone now. He's not going to war. He's much too young.'

Beatrice finally let Charlie go.

Angry with Beatrice for hurting him, Charlie shouted at the top of his voice as soon as he was released: 'Bang bang bang!' before running off.

'Come on, Gran,' Lucy said, 'let's get you home.'

Once they were inside her house, Beatrice sat down at the kitchen table and started to weep. Lucy wasn't sure what to do at first. Since they'd arrived in Devon she'd felt that she didn't know her gran at all. But as she looked at the old lady sobbing, Lucy's heart melted and she took her gran's hand.

'It's all right,' she said. 'It'll be all right.'

Beatrice barely seemed to hear her.

Charlie burst into the Fosters' farmhouse as Robert was finishing his letter to his mother and Mrs Foster was finishing her letter to Charlie's mother, telling her how well he'd been doing.

'Are you all right?' Robert asked Charlie.

Charlie opened his mouth and closed it again.

Robert reflected that Charlie really was a weird kid sometimes.

'If we hurry, these should make the last post,' Mrs Foster said.

'I'll take them.' Charlie took Mrs Foster's and Robert's letters and ran out of the door with them.

'We have to do something about Gran,' Lucy whispered to Robert when she got back, and she told him what had happened.

But Robert was ahead of her. He'd already written to their mum to ask her what they should do for the best.

*

165

The next day Beatrice came round to the Fosters' house. 'I'd like to speak to Mr Charlie Wilkes,' she said.

Charlie hoped she wasn't going to shake or pinch him again.

'I'm sorry,' Beatrice told him.

'What for?' Charlie asked her.

'I shouldn't have shook you.'

Charlie definitely agreed with her about that. 'Or pinched me,' he said. 'It hurt.'

'I was frightened,' Beatrice said.

'You were frightened?' Charlie thought she'd got it the wrong way round. *He* was the one who'd been frightened. 'What of?'

'That you'd go to war and be killed – like my son.'

'Oh.' Charlie took in what she'd said. 'So you were trying to protect me, sort of?'

'Exactly,' Beatrice said. 'Well, I can't stand here all day, I've got work to do.'

'Digging holes?' Charlie asked her.

Beatrice stared at him with a very odd look. 'Holes? What are you talking about?' she said.

At first when Buster was taken and the gunshot fired, Rose and Tiger stayed very still for a long time.

In the early hours of the morning they moved on.

A farmer taking his sheep to market had two stow-aways among his flock. Later, a lorry loaded with fish had two extra guests – and two less fish by the time it reached its destination.

But Rose and Tiger's journey was not the same as it had been when they'd had Buster with them. Without Buster's waggy tail and inquisitive nose, a large part of the joy had gone.

Once, Tiger spotted a Jack Russell ahead of them and raced down the street after it, only to discover that it wasn't Buster. He went back to Rose whose nose had told her already that it wasn't their friend but some other dog – one that didn't smell of the sea and rabbits and adventures on Salisbury Plain.

And then there was a new smell. At first it was so faint Rose hardly registered it, but it gradually grew stronger until it couldn't be ignored. It was the smell of sheep and moor ponies, Red Ruby Devon cattle and moorland heather. It was the smell of home.

Chapter 18

Lucy had waited so long for a reply to the now six letters she'd sent to Mrs Harris that finally she decided to ask about them at the Post Office, which doubled as the village shop. Inside, it was crammed to the brim with provisions and very busy as always. It wasn't just a place to buy groceries, but a place to catch up on the latest gossip.

As Lucy tried to decide between liquorice sticks, butterscotch sweets or aniseed balls from the small array of sweets beside the Pears soap and Rinso washing powder, she listened to what was being said around her.

'Like I said, I don't blame you for taking him home – it's not like there's been any bombs in London, has there?'

'Blasted phoney war – I'd take my young'un back . . .'

'They'll all have gone back to London before Christmas, you'll see.'

Lucy ran all the way home to tell Robert the news.

'So we didn't need to leave and the pets didn't need to go to the Harrises after all,' she gasped.

Robert took one of the aniseed balls from the paper bag Lucy offered him.

'Well, look on the bright side,' he said.

Lucy wasn't sure what he meant.

'We might get to go back home for Christmas too,' he grinned.

Lucy was particularly pleased when she got to school the next day and found that Pincher Jane had gone.

'Where's Jane?' she asked Amy, who usually sat next to Jane. 'Is she sick?'

'Her dad came and took her home,' Amy said.

'Oh,' said Lucy, although what she really wanted to do was dance around the room yelling with delight. 'I'll miss her.' Which was true; Lucy would certainly notice that Pincher Jane wasn't there any more.

At breaktime Amy sat by herself looking lonely, and over the next few days Lucy and Amy started to spend much more time together, until by the end of the week they were sitting next to each other in class and the best of friends.

On the same day that Charlie's mum received Charlie's letter, Mrs Edwards received a letter from Robert. It detailed his and Lucy's concerns about their grandmother. Mrs Edwards immediately took the letter to Sylvia, the matron of the hospital ship.

Mrs Edwards liked Sylvia; during her fifteen-year

career as a nurse she had worked for many matrons and Sylvia Carter was one of the best.

Sylvia seemed to get her staff to do all that needed doing and more, while always managing to make the work seem achievable. Sylvia's face wasn't naturally inclined to smile and she certainly wasn't interested in having friendly chats with Mrs Edwards or the volunteer nurses, but Mrs Edwards had a lot of respect for her.

'I'm not sure what I should do,' Mrs Edwards said, standing in front of Sylvia's desk while the matron read Robert's letter.

'Aren't you, Helen?' Sylvia said, looking up from the end of the letter. 'I think it's perfectly clear what you should do.'

Meanwhile Charlie's mum read his letter. She was missing him just as badly as Charlie was missing her, maybe even more so. She kept thinking how it wouldn't be a proper Christmas without her Charlie there. His billet mother down in Devon, Mrs Foster, had been very kind, keeping her informed of what was happening and how Charlie was getting on, but it wasn't the same as having her little boy with her. And when she received the letter with Charlie's addition on the back of the envelope, her mind was made up and she booked a train ticket down to Devon to fetch Charlie home.

Both women arrived in Devon the next day.

Helen Edwards was shocked at how dreadfully thin her mother was. There was nothing to her.

What's more, she felt guilty for expecting so much from her. How could she ever have imagined that Beatrice would be able to look after Robert and Lucy? Why hadn't she noticed just how frail Beatrice was when she went to her father's funeral?

'I'm sorry,' she told Beatrice. And she truly was.

Beatrice brushed her daughter's apology aside. 'You're here now, Helen,' she said. 'And that's all that matters. I miss my Bertie.'

'Oh, Mum,' Mrs Edwards said, taking her mother's hand.

It was more than twenty years ago – 1917 – and Mrs Edwards, or Helen Harper as she'd been then, had only been about Lucy's age when they'd learnt that Bertie had been killed at the front. She could still remember the terrible inhuman wailing sound that her mother had made on hearing the news. She remembered the nightmares she'd had as a child, reliving again and again the imagined horror of her brother's death. Later she'd come to realize that many of the soldiers who survived the war suffered just as much as those who'd died. Thousands of men came home from the Great War with mental problems. She'd seen them at the hospital where she'd trained. They'd experienced the misery and terror of life in the trenches, seeing their friends die and having to take the lives of their fellow men in battle. How could they just forget what they'd been through and go on with their everyday lives?

Helen tried to put these thoughts out of her head, and busied herself with unpacking her suitcase. She'd even brought William's slippers with her – silly fool, she berated herself, but she hadn't been able to leave them at home when her husband had forgotten to take them with him. She hugged his slippers to her and wished that the war would be over soon so that they could all be back together.

Mrs Foster was very surprised when she opened the door to a pale woman in town clothes, who looked vaguely familiar.

'May I help you?' she asked her.

'I've come to take my Charlie home,' the woman said.

'Oh – Charlie,' said Mrs Foster, realizing that the reason the woman looked familiar was that she must be Charlie's mother, or older sister. 'He's such a delightful –'

But the woman didn't let Mrs Foster finish.

'Where is he?'

'Well, he's at school –'

'Where's the school?' the woman interrupted her.

'About two miles down the lane.'

'I'd better take his things.'

'But – you're not thinking of taking Charlie away . . .'

Mrs Foster realized that that was exactly what the woman was thinking, and her heart sank.

'What else could I be expected to do after the way he's been treated?'

Mrs Foster was flabbergasted. 'Treated?'

Charlie's mother pulled the envelope out of her bag and showed Mrs Foster what Charlie had written on the back of it. 'I bin hurt bad.'

Now Mrs Foster understood. 'Oh . . . oh, it was all a misunderstanding.'

She tried to explain about Beatrice, but Charlie's mother was not in the mood to listen.

'Which direction is the school?'

Mrs Foster felt as though her heart was breaking. She was going to miss Charlie terribly. The little boy with the quirky, gap-toothed smile had wormed his way into her heart and would always have his own special place there.

She collected together Charlie's belongings.

'I can show you the way to the school . . .'

But Charlie's mum said she'd find it by herself.

'Why don't you stay here tonight and leave in the morning?' Her husband and Robert were out with the sheep. They wouldn't even get a chance to say goodbye to Charlie.

But Charlie's mum said they'd be leaving as soon as she'd collected Charlie from school.

At school Charlie was listening to his teacher telling them about a horse in the Trojan War and wishing that he hadn't already eaten his pasty, when the classroom door opened and Charlie could hardly believe his eyes.

'Mum!' He stumbled out of his chair, ran to her and threw his arms round her. 'Mum – it's my mum,' he told the rest of his class.

'Where are you going?' Lucy called to him when she saw Charlie heading out of the playground with a woman she didn't recognize.

'I'm going home,' Charlie told her, his face beaming.

Chapter 19

The two soldiers were very proud of their catch.
Sergeant Hooper had told them to get him the little
dog, and it hadn't been easy, but they'd managed to
track him through the woods and catch him.

'Come on, Rover.'

'We'll be in Sarge's good books for this.'

They carried Buster back to the camp in triumph
– only he was as wriggly as an eel and as awkward
as water to carry. Finally they knotted all four of
their bootlaces together and tied the rope round the
Jack Russell's neck; now he had to go with them
whether he wanted to or not!

'Come on, Rover. We need you for the war effort.'

There was a dearth of healthy dogs to help with
the war, due to thousands of them being killed in the
first few weeks of the war being announced. Once
the bombs started falling, dogs with good noses and
tracking instincts were going to be desperately needed
to help with the search and rescue of victims from
damaged buildings. There were woefully few dogs

now available, so few that the public was being asked to lend their pets to the war effort for the duration.

Adverts were appearing in national newspapers asking for people with suitable dogs to come forward.

Buster looked like an excellent candidate and their sergeant was a keen dog handler. As soon as he'd spotted Buster, he'd sent them after him.

Buster had gone quite a way and they'd almost given up by the time they found him down the rabbit hole.

The two soldiers had also shot at, but missed, the rabbit that Buster had been after.

'That rabbit would have made a nice change from bully beef,' they said, disgruntled.

They'd had bully beef, or corned beef as it was called on the tin, a lot since being posted to Salisbury. Bully beef stew, pie, fritters, even bully beef curry. A rabbit would have made a welcome change.

'So you caught him?' Sergeant Hooper said, nodding at Buster, when they got back.

'Yes, sir.'

'Give him something to eat then, and we'll see what he's made of.'

Buster was given a tin plate filled with bully beef, which he found most palatable. It was soon wolfed down and the plate licked clean.

Sergeant Hooper had been a circus dog trainer before he signed up. He began Buster's assessment as soon as Buster had finished his bully beef.

'Right – let's see what you're made of, dog. Sit!'

Buster immediately sat. Sergeant Hooper smiled.

'Down.'

Buster lay down.

'Stay.' Sergeant Hooper put his hand out flat in front of him, palm up, to reinforce his command. Sergeant Hooper walked away from him and then stopped.

'Come!'

Buster raced to him and sat down in front of him. 'Good, very good. You'd have made a good circus dog,' he told Buster.

Buster passed the initial assessment with flying colours. Now he'd need to go for more specialized training in Kent.

Sergeant Hooper sent a letter with the soldier that took Buster to Maidstone. 'This is one fine little dog. Please treat him with the respect he deserves. Sergeant D.M. Hooper. PS He'll do anything for a bit of bully beef.'

When Sam Malden went to meet their newest canine recruit at the station, he was very pleased when Buster wagged his tail as soon as they met and readily accepted a treat from him. Buster had just the right inquisitive and friendly temperament for the job.

Sam introduced Buster to the other dog handlers at the Kent centre straight away. Buster was the first potential search-and-rescue dog assigned to Sam that he was to be solely in charge of, and he was excited and nervous. Buster wasn't nervous at all. He was too busy being stroked and sniffing new friends. When he saw a collie, he raced over to it excitedly. But it wasn't Rose.

'What do you think of him, lad?' the corporal asked Sam.

'Think I'm already smitten,' Sam admitted.

'Remember, he's here to work.'

Sam didn't forget. But he didn't forget to make time to play with Buster either.

The other handlers commented on how well Buster and Sam worked together.

'It's like Patch knows what you're going to ask him to do even before you've said it, Sam.'

'Hardly have to teach him a thing – he just teaches himself.'

Buster excelled at agility training. The tunnels that he ran through weren't dissimilar to rabbit holes, and climbing the A-frame apparatus was a whole lot easier than chasing a squirrel up a tree.

'Your most important job is going to be to find people, Patch,' Sam told him. Buster wagged his tail.

As a first step Buster spent a lot of time finding his ball. Then he moved on to finding soldiers that were hiding in the tunnels and simulations of damaged buildings and rubble.

'Find him, Patch. Where is he?'

Sam was always really pleased with Buster when he successfully found the soldier. And Buster was always over the moon when Sam was pleased with him.

Finally there was scent training. Buster practised using his powerful canine nose to pick up the scent of a human in a collapsed building and alert Sam.

'One day you might need to find someone buried under rubble from a bomb and all you'll have is a smell to go on,' Sam said.

The pair worked hard until, two weeks later, Sam and Buster were called into the corporal's office.

'I've got a special job for you two.'

'Yes, sir?' Sam said. Buster wagged his tail.

'I need you to go to London and demonstrate what a search-and-rescue dog might be called on to do.'

'Us, sir?'

'Yes, and hopefully you'll encourage more people to loan their dogs to the war effort. Heaven knows we're going to need them when this thing really kicks off.'

Sam was so nervous the first time he and Buster did a demonstration that his hands were shaking and he felt sick.

Buster did everything Sam asked of him and captured the hearts of the audience as well.

'What a sweet little dog. Reminds me of my Toby,' a young girl said.

'He never takes his eyes off that handler of his,' commented her mother. 'And that's not like your Toby.'

Sam wasn't so nervous at their next demonstration because Buster had performed so well at the first one. He was even less nervous at the one after that. Their fourth demonstration was at the Wood Green Animal Shelter and one of the spectators was Michael.

He could hardly believe his eyes when he saw Buster. It couldn't be. But it had to be.

'Buster!' Michael shouted.

Buster looked over at Michael and his tail started wagging a million times a minute – and the next moment he'd run over and leapt into Michael's arms and was licking his face.

'Hey, hey, I already had a wash this morning,' Michael laughed, as Buster's little tongue got busy.

'You know him then?' Sam said.

'Oh yes, I know him,' Michael said. 'Buster's a friend of mine's dog.'

'Not any more,' Sam said. 'He's been conscripted for the war effort.'

Sam told Michael how Buster had been trained as a search-and-rescue dog. 'And he's one of the best they've seen so far.'

'He always was a smart little dog,' Michael said. More than anything, he was delighted that Buster was still alive.

Michael asked about Rose and Tiger, but Sam knew nothing about them.

'Even Patch – sorry, Buster – didn't come from round here. He was brought up from Somerset.'

Sam took Buster from Michael's arms.

'He's going to be fantastically helpful once the war really takes off over here,' Sam said.

'So you still believe it will?' Michael asked. Lots of people had stopped believing the war was ever going to come to Great Britain. Hitler was too busy overseas. Many of the children who had been evacuated in September were now home and looking forward to spending Christmas with their families.

'It will be here soon enough, believe me,' Sam said, 'and then we'll know all about it.'

'Dad, you won't believe what happened,' Michael told his father when he got home. His eyes were shining with excitement. He told him about spotting Buster. 'And he's a search-and-rescue dog. He didn't get killed, Dad.'

And if Buster hadn't been killed then there was a chance, albeit a slim one, that Rose and Tiger hadn't been killed either.

Mr Ward was pleased to see Michael more like himself again. There'd been an uncomfortable awkwardness between them over the past few weeks and Michael had barely spoken to him.

He'd tried to explain to Michael that they just couldn't save all the pets. 'It'd be impossible.'

But Michael flatly refused to accept that it was true. 'There's no reason any of them have to die.'

Nothing Mr Ward said would sway his son and he'd started to worry that choosing to keep Michael in London hadn't been such a wise idea. Having to report the pets Michael had been trying to save – that had been a terrible day for them both. He still hadn't told his son that it was he who had done it. But he thought Michael might suspect that it was.

Mr Ward had seen more than a few of the evacuated children back in London. He didn't blame the parents for bringing their children home for Christmas, even though he'd been criticized for keeping Michael in London. Not a single bomb had landed in Britain so far and there'd been no gas attacks.

'Does Buster get leave?' Michael's father asked.

'I don't see why not,' Michael said. Everyone else who'd been conscripted did.

'Maybe you'd like to take him down to Devon for a few days, see your friends. Get to tell them Buster's story in person. I'm sure it could be arranged.'

Michael hadn't been in touch with Robert since the day the pets he'd been trying to save had been taken away. He'd felt too ashamed to tell anyone what had happened and blamed himself for putting the animals in danger. For weeks afterwards he'd looked for them and tried to find some clue as to where they'd been taken. He'd gone to every animal shelter he knew of, but finally he had had to accept that he wasn't going to find them.

It'd be a lot easier to tell Robert and Lucy that he didn't know what had happened to Rose and Tiger either if he had Buster with him.

Chapter 20

Tiger, for all that he'd been a town cat his whole life, was now in his element as he and Rose hunted on the moors together.

His sleek frame leapt on unsuspecting frogs, raced across the heather after rabbits and basked in any faint glimmer of winter sunshine that he could find.

Rose had been taught to avoid the adder and grass snakes that lived on the moors from the time she was a young puppy. But Tiger had never even seen a snake before and when he saw the black and grey zigzag-patterned snake basking in the winter sunshine on top of the moorland heather, he was intrigued rather than wary of it. Slowly, so slowly, he edged towards it – ready to pounce at the perfect moment.

He was just about to leap when Rose raced towards him, knocking him over and sending him flying. Tiger yeowled and hissed at the dog. Then he turned back to his prey, but it was too late – the adder had gone.

As the days passed, the last of the winter sunshine faded. All too soon the winds on the moor turned bitterly cold, and freezing rain drenched them almost daily.

At the end of one particularly bad day they found a disused barn and slunk inside. Rose flopped on the ground, exhausted from the day's hunting with its meagre catch. Tiger lay down beside her, his furry side pressed against her flank for warmth.

Outside it started to snow, lightly at first, the white flakes floating softly down. But as Rose and Tiger slept on, it grew heavier until it had turned into a blizzard and other animals came into the barn to get away from the snow.

Tiger kept very very still when he felt warm breath on him, only opening his eyes when he felt it lessen. Hay had been left in a horse trough on the wall for the moor ponies, should they need it during the winter. Above Tiger a nut-brown pony lifted his head and tugged hungrily at it.

'Driven through worse than this,' the fish-truck driver told Michael, as he skidded round the treacherous corner of a narrow Devonshire lane and past a disused barn.

Michael held firmly on to Buster, who was sitting on his lap.

'Good dog.'

Buster panted. The smell of the fish was so tantalizing

to his sensitive nose that he was almost drooling. They'd been travelling for hours and he still hadn't been given any.

The driver pressed on down the winding country lanes. Michael's father had asked him to take the boy and his dog down to Devon, paid him a bit too – and he always made his deliveries, whatever the weather.

Buster looked out of the window at the unrelenting snow. After hours of driving through treacherous conditions, they finally reached Robert and Lucy's grandmother's house.

'Come in, have a cup of tea at least, to warm you up,' Helen told the fish-truck driver. He thanked her, but said he'd rather be on his way, as fish waited for no one.

Robert and Lucy were overjoyed to see Buster and he went crazy when he saw them, circling round and round and jumping up at them.

'But where are Rose and Tiger?' Lucy asked. 'Didn't you bring them?'

Michael shook his head.

'Aren't they with the Harrises still?' Helen said.

'No.'

Over a sandwich and a cup of tea for him and some scrambled freshly laid eggs for Buster, Michael told them all that he knew.

'So what can have happened to them?'

'Do you think they're still alive?'

'They can't be,' Lucy said, and a tear slipped down

her face. All this time, while they'd been down in Devon, thinking their pets were safe, they hadn't been safe at all. 'But how did Buster end up in Somerset?'

Michael didn't know.

'Poor Rose and Tiger.'

'There's still a chance,' Michael said.

Lucy and Robert nodded, but neither of them really believed that Rose and Tiger could be alive any more.

They sat in uneasy silence.

Buster had finished his scrambled eggs and was now looking hopefully at Michael's half-eaten sandwich.

Michael broke a bit off it and Buster gobbled it up, and then eyed the rest of the sandwich. When Michael didn't give him any, he put out a paw and touched Michael's leg, then looked pointedly at the sandwich and gave a whine. He couldn't have been clearer about what he wanted.

Robert and Lucy laughed in spite of themselves.

Michael gave Buster the rest of his sandwich.

'It's impossible to resist him!' Robert said.

'Buster's got to be back in London for New Year,' Michael told them. 'They call him Patch, and they need him to encourage more people to allow their dogs to become search-and-rescue dogs.'

'He's Buster, not Patch,' Lucy said firmly. 'As soon as the war's over, we want him back as our pet.'

'Might even come back with a medal, mightn't you, Buster?' Robert said.

Buster hopped up into Robert's lap.

'What's that dog doing in this house?' Beatrice said from the doorway. She didn't sound pleased to see him.

'This is Buster, Mother,' Helen said. 'One of our pets from London.'

'I don't care if he's the King's Corgi, Dookie. No dog is welcome in this house.'

'But, Gran,' Robert said. His grandmother could be so infuriating sometimes.

'Fleas and diseases, not in this house.'

'Michael's travelled all the way down from London with him.'

'He can sleep in the barn like Rose used to.'

'Buster's helping with the war effort,' Lucy said.

'Good for him. A dog's place is outside.'

Nothing they said could persuade Beatrice otherwise. But they didn't want Buster to have to spend the night outside.

Robert and Michael pulled on their coats.

'Watch out for holes,' Robert said, as they went through the yard. 'Gran's been digging them all over the place.' He pointed to a particularly large one.

Robert and Michael trudged through the snow with Buster to the Fosters' house. Before they'd even reached the front door Molly came racing over to greet them. Buster's tail was wagging nineteen to the dozen as he said hello to this promising-looking new friend.

Mr Foster opened the front door and Buster ran inside, with Molly slipping in behind him before Mr Foster could stop her.

'Well, look at that,' Mrs Foster laughed, as the two dogs made themselves comfortable in front of the roaring fire. 'Molly's never even tried to come in the house before and now she acts as though she's in here all the time.'

Mr Foster shook Michael's hand and while Robert told him about his gran's refusal to let Buster into the house, Mr Foster took Michael's coat and suitcase and said Michael and Buster were more than welcome to stay with them.

Robert was mortified by his gran's behaviour.

'I'm so sorry,' he said to Michael.

But Michael brushed the apology aside. 'Buster doesn't mind.'

And Buster certainly didn't seem to mind. It was as though he and Molly had been friends forever rather than friends who'd just met.

After giving Michael and Buster some supper, Mrs Foster took Michael up to Robert and Charlie's old room, while Robert trudged back to his gran's. At least the snow had stopped falling, although it was still thick on the ground.

Back at the Fosters', Buster and Molly slept

together all night by the fire and woke next morning to a white-covered farmyard, signalling a whole new day of fun in the snow.

Chapter 21

Christmas Day began for Robert and Lucy with stockings filled with an orange, a small bar of chocolate, some pencils and hankies, which their mother had left at the ends of their beds. They were grateful that rationing hadn't started yet as they each gobbled a piece of chocolate before breakfast – the only day such a treat was allowed.

'I could eat chocolate for breakfast every day,' Robert announced as everyone wished each other Merry Christmas.

'I'm sure you could,' said his mother, smiling.

'What do you think Dad is having for breakfast?' asked Robert.

His mother tried not to look sad – everyone wished he was with them on today of all days. 'Oh, a delicious breakfast with bacon and eggs just how he likes them . . . and chocolate, of course!'

Robert and Lucy felt better after that. They knew their father probably wasn't having chocolate, or bacon and eggs for that matter, but if they could imagine it then so it was, for now.

After she got dressed, Lucy headed out into the snowy winter morning. She didn't like using the outside toilet at her gran's. Big black spiders lurked on the walls and after all the snow she had to break the ice off the door latch to get in.

Worse, Gran's yard was now more of a hazard than ever because the snow had covered up most of the holes Gran had been digging. If you weren't careful you could easily get your foot stuck down one.

Beatrice insisted they all go to the early morning carol service, and after that they headed over to the Fosters' farm.

Buster was very excited to see them, and immediately wanted Robert to throw a ball for him and his new friend, Molly.

'I've been throwing it all morning,' Michael told Robert and Lucy. 'They never seem to have enough of playing with it.'

Buster dropped the ball at Robert's feet, then sat down and looked up at him hopefully, his head cocked to one side. Molly stood behind Buster and wagged her tail.

Robert really had no choice. He threw the ball, and the two dogs chased after it and brought it back to him to be thrown again.

Mrs Foster made Christmas dinner for everyone

at her house and gave Lucy and Robert the jumpers she'd knitted for them.

Lucy gave Mr and Mrs Foster the hats she'd been making.

Pride of place on the Fosters' mantelpiece was given to a hand-drawn, slightly grubby Christmas card of what might have been a Devon Ruby cow wearing a red Santa Claus hat – though it was hard to tell.

His mum had put a note inside it to say that Charlie had explained what had happened, and how grateful she was for all that Mr and Mrs Foster had done for her son.

'Merry Christmas' Charlie had carefully traced over the greeting, and then added: 'Bin missing the pasties love your Charlie xxx'

In London a telegram messenger pulled up outside the floating hospital as it lay at its berth. Spotting him from the window, the matron drew herself up, steeling herself to put a brave face forward, however bad the news might be. She thought that the men who brought the telegrams to people to tell them their loved ones were dead or missing in action probably had one of the worst jobs of the war. No one wanted to see them. People would run into their homes at the sound of their motorbike engines, hoping that the message wouldn't be for them. She hurried to the entrance of the boat, praying that her husband was safe.

'May I help you?' she started to say as the messenger approached.

But then she saw who the messenger was. Their first and only river rescue – Private Matthews!

Sylvia felt all the tension within her release. She laughed as she hugged the surprised man to her. Not bad news after all. Just a friend come to see them and let them all know how he was getting on.

'Merry Christmas, and how are you?' she asked him.

'Fine, fine . . .' Something in his voice was wrong. 'Only I hate to be the one to bring it, after she was so good to me, and on today of all days.'

Sylvia saw the telegram he was holding, which he'd shielded from being squashed by the impromptu hug. She let go of him like he had the plague.

The telegram was addressed to Mrs Helen Edwards.

'Better to know than not to know, isn't it?' Private Matthews said, his eyes asking Sylvia to tell him that he'd done the right thing.

But Sylvia wasn't always sure that it was better to know, if it was bad news. Sometimes ignorance, as the saying went, could be bliss.

After Private Matthews had gone, Sylvia stared at the telegram for a long time. It was Christmas Day. Helen would be busy looking after her mother and the children. Would it really matter if she didn't receive her bad news telegram immediately? Sylvia didn't think it would. Decision made, she opened the top drawer of her desk and put the telegram inside it.

At 3 p.m. everyone crowded round the Fosters' wireless to listen to King George VI give his Christmas broadcast on the wireless.

'A new year is at hand. We cannot tell what it will bring. If it brings peace, how thankful we shall all be.'

Tears slipped down Beatrice's face as Lucy held her gran's hand.

'If it brings us continued struggle, we shall remain undaunted . . .'

After the broadcast they played Christmas party games and Lucy won musical chairs three times in a row – in spite of Buster and Molly trying to join in by running around and barking.

They could have stayed longer, but by early evening Helen could see Beatrice was exhausted.

'Time to go home, Mother.'

'You're welcome to stay here for the night,' Mrs Foster said. 'Rather than going back into the snow.'

'I've slept in my own bed for fifty years,' Beatrice said. 'I couldn't fall asleep anywhere else.'

'Get your coats, Robert and Lucy,' Helen said.

'But what about Buster?' Lucy said.

'He's staying here. You'll see him in the morning.'

'Don't worry – I'll take good care of him,' Michael said.

Buster and Molly were curled up together on the rug, the best of friends.

'Dogs shouldn't be allowed in the house,' Beatrice said disapprovingly. 'Rose knew her place – in the barn with the other farm animals.'

'But it's so cold out there,' Lucy said, feeling sorry for Rose. At least she'd been able to sleep indoors at their house in London.

Beatrice yawned widely.

'Let's get you to bed, Mother,' Helen said.

Mrs Foster came out of the kitchen carrying a cake tin.

'Bit of Christmas cake to take back with you,' she said.

'Thank you.'

'That was fine cake,' Beatrice said.

Robert and Lucy, Helen and Beatrice trudged back down the hill through the snow, with Beatrice insisting on carrying the cake tin.

The heavy snow had made travelling impossible for the last few days. So Rose and Tiger had shared the barn with the ponies and at night lay down together to sleep.

The hay that had been left for the ponies had also brought rats and mice to the barn, so they hadn't gone hungry.

Now it was time to move on and the two animals picked their way across the snow-laden moor. The hardy moor sheep stared at Tiger as they chewed on the remnants of grass, and turned their heads to watch him some more as he went past, chewing all the while.

As the light faded at the end of the day, Rose and Tiger would normally have found somewhere safe and out of the weather for the night. But tonight Rose pressed on and whined when Tiger would have stopped.

She padded through a gap in a drystone wall and made a strange sound in her throat. It was a sound that Tiger had never heard before. It was almost a hum.

The air here felt different to Rose, the air here smelt different. It was the smell of almost-home.

Rose's tail wagged as she broke into a trot and Tiger ran after his friend.

They were still quite a long way from the farm when Rose's sensitive nose picked up the acrid tang of smoke. This was a very different smell: the smell of danger and death. Animals instinctively know to head away from fire rather than towards it.

Rose ran onwards in the direction of the fire, however, and Tiger, after hesitating for a moment, ran after her.

Michael was fast asleep when Buster woke him by barking and then jumping on the bed and pulling at the covers.

'What is it? What's wrong?' Michael said.

Buster jumped off the bed, but kept on barking.

The noise woke Mr Foster and he came to Michael's room. 'What's got into him?' he said, as he opened the door.

As soon as the door was opened, Buster shot out of it.

Michael headed after him. 'I don't know,' he said to Mr Foster. 'But he's a trained search-and-rescue dog – he wouldn't be barking for no reason.'

Buster was now barking by the front door. Molly stood next to him, not sure what was happening.

Mr Foster pulled the front door open and Buster raced outside, barking and barking.

Now they didn't need Buster to tell them something was wrong. They could see it for themselves, and smell it too.

'Fire!' Mr Foster cried.

In the valley below them, where Beatrice's house was, they could see the flicker of orange flames.

Mr Foster ran to his truck, with Michael and Buster right behind him.

Robert's first thought was that a bomb had hit the house. He threw off the bedclothes, ran into Lucy's room and dragged her out of bed.

'Wh-what is it?'

'Come on!'

Helen ran out of her room at the same time, wearing her dressing-gown and her husband's slippers. She ran to Beatrice's room. The door was open and the room empty. Her mother must have already got out.

She hurried Robert and Lucy down the stairs and out into the yard.

They were only just in time; the fire had taken hold in some of the rooms downstairs and it was burning wildly.

'Where's Gran?' Lucy said.

Helen looked around. Beatrice's room had been empty. She had to be outside.

'Wait here,' she told Robert and Lucy. 'Mum . . . Mother!' she called out, as she went to look for her.

A black shadow ran past Robert and Lucy and into the house.

'That looked like . . . Rose!' Lucy said.

'It couldn't be, could it?' said Robert.

Inside the burning building, Rose found Beatrice in the kitchen where the fire was raging. The elderly lady had been overcome by smoke and had collapsed on the floor.

'Shouldn't be in here . . .' Beatrice muttered, as Rose started to drag her out by her dressing-gown. The old lady was thin, but she was still very heavy for a collie to pull across the floor, even one as determined as Rose.

Doggedly, Rose clamped her teeth more firmly

round the dressing-gown material. She wouldn't give up.

'No!' Helen screamed when she saw Robert running towards the house.

Robert grabbed an old rag that was hanging on a nail by the door, wet with frost, and covered his nose and mouth with it. But as soon as he went back into the house he knew he couldn't stay for long. Smoke was everywhere. Crawling on his hands and knees, he shouted out, 'Rose!' From the kitchen he thought he heard a bark. He crawled over and pushed the door open with his foot. Through the haze he could see the figure of a dog and a body slumped on the ground, but the smoke was getting thicker by the second.

'Gran!'

When she saw Robert, Rose wagged her tail, but she didn't stop trying to drag Beatrice out of the kitchen.

'Good girl, Rose,' Robert said.

He quickly pulled Beatrice to her feet, put her right arm round his shoulder and his left arm round her waist.

'Bertie – Bertie, you came back,' Beatrice said. Robert half lifted and half dragged his grandmother outside as the flames finally engulfed the kitchen.

Mrs Edwards took her confused mother from Robert as Mr Foster's truck squealed to a halt.

'Where's my warm milk?' Beatrice demanded to

know. 'It's heating up on the stove. I want my warm milk with a slice of Christmas cake.'

'Where's Rose?' Robert said. She'd been right behind him.

'I knew it was her!' said Lucy. She burst into tears as she stared at the burning cottage.

'No dogs in the house,' Gran insisted, as flames consumed the door she and Robert had just come out of.

Robert pulled his dressing-gown over his head, ready to go back in.

'No!' Helen cried, grabbing his arm tight. 'You'll get yourself killed. Whatever dog that was, it wasn't Rose, and it won't stand a chance now. Look at it.'

The house was an inferno. Lucy sobbed, as Helen hugged her to her.

Buster jumped from the Fosters' truck, and raced across the yard towards a shape on the ground, barking and barking.

Michael ran after him and found a collie lying on her side in the snow. It looked as though she'd managed to get out through the small side window. But she wasn't moving. He carefully picked her up and carried her away from the house, which he was worried might collapse at any moment.

'It *is* Rose!' Lucy exclaimed, running up to him. Rose was very still. 'Is she – is she . . .?' But she couldn't say the word 'dead'.

Michael put Rose down on the ground and

listened to her heart, then put his mouth over Rose's nose and exhaled into her, forcing air through her nose and into her lungs as he'd been taught at NARPAC.

Come on, he silently begged.

Everyone else, besides Buster, who was digging across the yard, gathered round and watched and waited.

Michael listened to Rose's heart and then repeated the breathing.

'She moved!' Lucy cried. 'She moved!'

She was right – Rose was breathing again. At the sound of Lucy's voice she lifted and dropped her tail, and Lucy crouched down beside her in the snow and sobbed.

'We have to get her into the warmth as soon as possible,' Michael said, looking serious. 'She won't survive if she stays out here.'

'Let's take her back to our house,' Mr Foster said, and he wrapped Rose up in some sacking and lifted her into the back of the truck where Michael and Lucy cradled her.

'Buster – come on!' Robert yelled.

Buster was digging at a large snow-clogged hole close to the burning house as though his life depended upon it.

Robert raced over to him and dragged him away by his collar, but as soon as he let go Buster ran back and started digging again.

'Buster, come here!' Robert went back and peered into the hole, trying to work out what was so important.

Staring up at him, looking pitiful but unharmed, was a familiar face. 'Tiger? What are you doing here?' Robert lifted the bedraggled ginger furball out and hugged him to him. The cat smelt terrible, but Tiger was definitely alive.

'You OK?' Michael asked him, as Robert ran back to the truck with Buster and Tiger and climbed in.

'Look who I found,' Robert said.

'Tiger!' squealed Lucy in disbelief.

'How on earth did they get here?' asked Helen, too confused to even think about it.

'Maybe they missed us as much as we missed them,' Lucy said, as she stroked the cat. Tiger rubbed his head against her.

Jumping up on his hind legs from the foot space, Buster licked Tiger's face, then pawed over to where Rose lay on Michael's lap beside Lucy. The Jack Russell squeezed down between Rose and Tiger, whining softly as the collie's wheezing breaths filled the space around them.

Chapter 22

Over the next few days everyone kept a careful watch on Rose as she steadily got better. Tiger and Buster barely left her side unless they were forced to. Buster bolted down his food and then raced back to her. Tiger lay curled up close to her during the day, but curled up with Lucy in her bed at night.

Poor Molly was confused. She tried to play with Buster, but he wouldn't play, so she tried to play with Tiger, but Tiger gave a miaow that let her know in no uncertain terms that it wasn't the time for playing.

Robert and Lucy and Michael spent all of their time with Rose too. None of the children could believe that the pets were all safe and well. They tried to work out how they could have got to them, but it seemed impossible.

'Only Rose has ever lived down here before.'

'Rose is pretty determined,' Mrs Foster said. 'Even as a puppy you could see she was a dog with a strong character.'

While Michael stayed with the pets, Robert and Lucy went with their mother and Gran to see what could be salvaged of Beatrice's property and bring back the chickens, none of which seemed to be any the worse for their smoky ordeal.

Beatrice almost stumbled into one of the holes that were all over the yard.

'Someone should fill these in,' she said crossly. 'They're a health hazard.'

Robert and Lucy smiled.

When Rose was fit again, Mr Foster and Robert took her out to the sheep, while Michael and Lucy took Buster and Molly for a walk.

'Do you think she'll remember what she's supposed to do?' Robert asked Mr Foster.

Mr Foster blew the whistle twice – one shorter and one longer blast – the command for 'come-bye'.

Rose looked first at Mr Foster and then at Robert. She wagged her tail.

'Go on then, Rose,' Robert said, and Rose ran off to do what she was born to do, moving round the sheep in a clockwise direction.

She'd forgotten none of her training and was in her element as she and Mr Foster worked the sheep, bringing them safely into their pen.

As Robert watched Rose obeying the commands that Mr Foster shouted, he could see she was at home here. A sheepdog through and through, she was back where she belonged.

At the end of an hour Mr Foster blew the whistle three times and Rose ran to him as she was supposed to do.

Mr Foster couldn't praise her enough. 'You're one fine dog,' he said. 'One very fine dog.'

Robert had never seen Rose's tail wag as hard as it did that day.

Back at the farmhouse Molly dropped her ball at Robert's feet while Rose followed Mr Foster.

'It's like . . .' Lucy started to say and stopped.

'Like what?'

'Like Rose is finally truly happy. It's like she's where she belongs.'

'What will you do with Molly now?' Robert asked Mr Foster. One thing that was clear to see and only highlighted more now that Rose was here, was that Molly was anything but a natural born sheepdog.

Mr Foster smiled. 'Well, if the war doesn't get going over here . . .'

Although war had been declared and officially started, and was very much under way in Europe, Britain had so far not been attacked.

'. . . Then maybe you'd like to do a swap – my Molly for your Rose?'

'I don't want Rose to have to sleep outside,' Lucy said.

'Oh, don't you worry about that – she'll have a

choice place by the fire,' Mrs Foster told her, and Lucy smiled.

It was almost midnight on New Year's Eve and everyone – aside from Beatrice, who'd gone to bed at nine – was still up. Lucy was almost asleep on the sofa, with Tiger curled up beside her. Molly and Rose were lying back to back by the roaring fire. Robert and Michael played marbles on the rug, with Buster lying slightly in their way, and the adults were talking softly about the war.

Suddenly Buster sat up, his head cocked to one side. He whined.

'What is it, boy?' Robert said.

Buster ran out of the room.

Robert stood up and followed him. He was just in time to see Buster racing up the stairs.

'Buster?'

A moment later the little dog came running back down with a brown, only slightly damaged, leather slipper in his mouth.

Robert went to take it from him when there was a knock at the front door behind them. Robert turned and opened it, only to have Buster rush past him, his tail wagging as hard as it could.

'Hello, Buster. Nice to see nothing's changed around here,' William said, taking his slipper from the dog.

Robert could hardly believe his eyes.

'It's Dad!' he shouted, and everyone came running.

As the clock struck midnight and the New Year began, William told them all that had happened and how he and his crew had been saved by a homing pigeon named Lily.

'Joe sent her back to the airfield with grid coordinates and they were able to send out a rescue party and pick us up. Without Lily – well, let's say I might not have been home yet.' William smiled, as he squeezed Helen's hand and hugged Lucy to him.

Britain's battle in the sky was already in progress, and on land it was about to begin in earnest, but for tonight his family were together and safe.

Tiger twirled round his legs and William lifted him on to his lap and buried his face in his soft ginger-and-white fur. He was so glad to be back with his family.

Lucy stroked Rose sitting beside her as Buster picked up the ball he and Molly had been playing with earlier. He padded over to Michael and dropped the ball at his feet, looked at it and then looked up at Michael. Molly wagged her tail hopefully.

Robert laughed. Buster and Molly were being perfectly clear about what they wanted. 'Come on then,' he said, and they all went out into the star-filled moonlit night. It was time for the first game of the New Year.

Afterword

A little-known historical fact sets the scene for this book: in September 1939, after the announcement that Great Britain was at war, more than 400,000 cats and dogs were put down at their owners' request in just four days. Between 1939 and 1940, another 350,000 pets were killed.

The total number of pets that were put down – 750,000 – is more than twelve-and-a-half times the number of civilian deaths throughout the country during the whole of the Second World War.

The Dickin Medal is awarded to animals for 'acts of conspicuous gallantry and devotion to duty in wartime'. The medal was instituted in 1943 and named after the PDSA founder, Mrs Maria Dickin CBE.

During the Second World War, a total of 54 Dickin Medals were awarded, of which 32 went to pigeons, 18 to dogs, three to horses and one to a cat.

In 2004 a memorial to commemorate all the

animals and birds that were killed during wartime was erected in Hyde Park. Pigeons were given pride of place on the wall of the sculpture and carved in relief.

Around 250,000 homing pigeons were used during the Second World War.

Winston Churchill's fondness for cats is well documented. For his 88th birthday he was given a ginger cat that he named Jock. After Churchill's death his family asked that a marmalade cat always be resident at Chartwell. In November 2010 Jock number 5, a kitten who'd been rescued by Cats Protection, moved in. He has an unlikely love of water.

Acknowledgements

Huge thanks to the many, many people and places that helped in the researching of this book. The personal stories were moving and enlightening, and special thanks go to Terry and Shirley Bender and George and Angela Moore. Also to Barnstaple and Tiverton museums for their help with the Devon research, and no book on the war would be complete without a visit to the Imperial War Museum. The staff at the Twinwood Airfield Museum gave a fascinating insight into life in the RAF in the Second World War.

On the writing side I would like to thank my agent Clare Pearson, of Eddison Pearson, whose encouragement and support were invaluable, and my editor at Puffin, Shannon Park, whose brilliant idea this book was. Also Samantha Mackintosh and Marcus J. Fletcher – copy-editors extraordinaire – who I hope I'm lucky enough to work with on future books.

Thanks to Emily Cox at Puffin whose real Tiger inspired the fictional one, Andrea Norfolk for her invaluable information about collies and Lynda White whose own Jack Russells, Buster and Lily, are quite different from Buster in the story.

Finally, thanks to my own two dogs, Traffy and Bella, who had to put up with shorter walks during the writing of this book and are looking forward to some very long walks to make up for it. And as always, my husband, who loved the book idea from the beginning and spent hours helping with the research, and suggested a trip to Devon that included a journey on the Somerset steam railway (with our dogs) that inspired Buster, Rose and Tiger's trip.

There are many heroes in war and some of them have four legs and some have wings.

megan rix

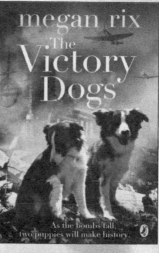

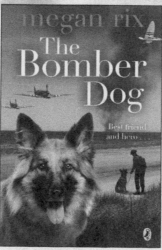

Find out more about Megan and her books at
www.meganrix.com

Bright and shiny and sizzling with fun stuff ...

puffin.co.uk

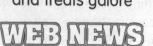

WEB CHAT

Discover something new
EVERY month – books, competitions and treats galore

WEB NEWS

The **Puffin Blog** is packed with posts and photos from Puffin HQ and special guest bloggers. You can also sign up to our monthly newsletter **Puffin Beak Speak**

WEB FUN

Take a sneaky peek around your favourite **author's studio**, une in to the **podcast**, **download activities** and much more

WEBBED FEET

(Puffins have funny little feet and brightly coloured beaks)

nt your mouse our way today!

It all started with a Scarecrow.

Puffin is seventy years old.
Sounds ancient, doesn't it? But Puffin has never been
so lively. We're always on the lookout for the next big
idea, which is how it began all those years ago.

Penguin Books was a big idea from the mind of
a man called Allen Lane, who in 1935 invented
the quality paperback and changed the world.
**And from great Penguins, great Puffins grew,
changing the face of children's books forever.**

The first four Puffin Picture Books were hatched in 1940 and the
first Puffin story book featured a man with broomstick arms called
Worzel Gummidge. In 1967 Kaye Webb, Puffin Editor, started the
Puffin Club, promising to **'make children into readers'**.
She kept that promise and over 200,000 children became
devoted Puffineers through their quarterly instalments of
Puffin Post, which is now back for a new generation.

Many years from now, we hope you'll look back and
remember Puffin with a smile. **No matter what your age
or what you're into, there's a Puffin for everyone.**
The possibilities are endless, but one thing is for sure:
whether it's a picture book or a paperback, a sticker book
or a hardback, **if it's got that little Puffin
on it – it's bound to be good.**